KNOCKED UP BY THE BILLIONAIRE'S SON

A SECRET BABY ROMANCE

LILIAN MONROE

Copyright © 2018 Lilian Monroe All rights reserved.

No part of this book may be reproduced or transmitted in any form or by any means without prior written permission from the author except for short quotations used for the purpose of reviews.

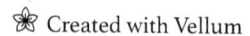

❦ Created with Vellum

1

DEAN

"Sorry for the late notice, Dean, but Jeremy's called in sick. We need you for two-year-old twins' birthday party tomorrow morning at 10am."

"Saturday is supposed to be my day off, Pat," I sigh. What was supposed to be a side job to give back to the community is turning into a massive time commitment.

"I know, buddy. Just help me out here. It's a cash job at a nice house, it'll pay for at least three of our non-profit events."

"Yeah, fine. No worries. Text me the address."

I hang up the phone and let out another sigh. I was looking forward to a day to myself tomorrow, but I can't back out now. It's not like I need the money, I've got loads of that. I met Pat at my niece's birthday party and found out he runs a non-profit organization for kids. I convinced him to give me a job as a children's entertainer, since working at my father's investment firm isn't exactly fulfilling. When he first offered me the job I'd laughed. 'Children's entertainer' is just a fancy way of saying 'clown'. I fell in love with the job right away, and now I love calling myself Clifford the Clown on the weekends.

I head to my closet and pull out the plastic dry-cleaner's bag hanging at the back. I unzip it and make sure everything is okay. The bright yellow suit has blue polka dots all over it with big red buttons down the front. I lay it down on my bed and pull out the suitcase with the rest of my costume and props in it. There are more than enough balloons and streamers, so all I have to do is make sure all my gear is ready to go for the morning.

It's surprisingly calming to get ready. I make sure everything is laid out for my costume and that I have enough face paint. I lay out all my balloons and games and pack them away neatly, and then I check my compressed air canister to make sure I'll be able to make balloon animals. Everything is just about in order when my phone rings again.

This better not be Pat cancelling the gig on me, I think to myself. It wouldn't be the first time it happens. As much as I love the guy and I respect what he's doing, he's not the most organized manager I've ever had. That's what you get when you work for a clown, I guess.

I pick up my phone and grimace. It's not Pat, it's worse. It's my mother.

"Mother," I say as I answer the phone.

"Dean, darling, how are you?" she asks in her honey-sweet voice.

"I'm fine, mom. What's up?"

"I just wanted to see how you were doing. I haven't spoken to you since the fundraiser last month."

Yeah, that wasn't by accident.

"I've been busy, mother. I'm doing this non-profit gig for the children's foundation."

"Of course, honey. The clown thing." I can almost hear her waving her hand dismissively. "I just wanted to call and see if you'd spoken to Victoria lately?"

A shiver runs down my spine and I shake my head. I take a deep breath before answering and force my voice to stay even.

"Victoria and I broke up two months ago, mother. You know that."

"I know, honey, it's just that your father and I liked her so much. And the Erkharts have been so good to us over the years. It seems like a shame to throw away such a great relationship over some silliness."

Silliness?! I bristle, and take another deep breath to calm myself. As usual, my mother is only thinking of herself. Never mind my heartbreak or my feelings. They wouldn't matter to her. She only cares about the contacts that the Erkharts bring to their investment business.

"We broke up," I repeat. "It's over."

"Talk to her, honey," she says. I wish she'd stop calling me that. "They were over for dinner the other day and she is so *sorry* for everything that happened. She said she's just worried about you, and she's ready to forgive you for storming out on her."

"SHE is ready to forgive ME?!" I almost shout. I hear a sharp intake of breath and I try my best to stay calm. Why did my mother have my ex-fiancée over for dinner anyways?! "We broke up. It's over."

"Talk to her, honey."

"Stop calling me honey," I snap.

My mother sighs. Her voice is harder when she speaks again . "You've caused us a world of pain with this breakup. Your union with Victoria was planned from the time you were two years old. We had millions tied into it. It's in your *best interest* to reconsider."

A chill goes down my spine and I resist the urge to fling my phone out the window.

"I think you're mistaking YOUR best interest with MY best interest," I spit back. *Typical of my mother, I shouldn't be surprised.* "I need to get ready for work."

"You need to get ready to put on a costume and blow up balloons, you mean," she snarls. "When are you going to grow up and realize where you come from. The only reason you're able to 'give back' is because of the sacrifices that your father and I made for you. You would have nothing without us."

"I'd have my integrity," I snap.

My mother snorts. "Right," she says. "Well, go get ready for your little job then. Call Victoria."

The phone clicks and this time I do fling it across the room. It lands on the sofa and bounces onto the floor as I put my hands against the wall and take deep breaths. I pull my arm back and smack the wall as hard as I can with my palm as a yell erupts out of me.

Why can't she understand that Victoria and I broke up? I walked in on her with another man in our own bed and she calls it 'silliness'?! What universe does she live in??

With another deep breath I try to calm myself down. I go back to my bedroom and zip up the plastic bag with my costume in it and lay it across the armchair in the corner. I look at the rainbow-colored wig and the red nose in the box beside the costume and I shake my head.

What am I doing? I'm dressing up as a clown and making balloon animals on the weekends instead of putting in extra hours at the investment firm with my father. My parents tolerated the time away when I was playing by the rules, but now I can sense their patience wearing thin.

I turn back around and stomp out into the living room. The New York skyline is glittering below me and I slump down in the sofa and put my head in my hand.

As much as I hate to admit it, my mother is right. I'm living in this penthouse because of them, and I can afford to work as a children's entertainer because of the trust fund that they set up for me. I owe them everything, but asking me to patch things up with Victoria Erkhart is just too much.

They'd never cut me off, would they? Not because I refused to marry the woman they chose for me? Surely they love me more than that?

2

SAMANTHA

THE PLANE LANDS in New York and I glance out the window. Dusk is starting to settle and the sky is ablaze with colors. I'm like a zombie, going through the motions without really thinking about what I'm doing. Before I know it, I'm loading my bag into the back of a taxi and giving the driver Jess's address.

I glance at my big purse and see the blue manila folder sticking out of it. I turn back to the window, trying to blink back the tears that have gathered in my eyes.

Divorced.

God, I hate that word.

Or rather, soon to be divorced. As soon as I sign on the dotted line it'll be official.

The buildings rush by us and I stare through the window without seeing anything. We're on a freeway, and then we're winding through streets with tall houses all stuck together. It looks just like the movies.

It's not until the taxi driver stops the car that I blink and take a deep breath, waking up from my daze. I pay the driver and carry my suitcase up the half dozen steps to my best friend's front door. My arm is just lifting to knock on the door when it swings open.

"Sam!" she exclaims. I can't help but smile.

"Hi, Jess."

"Come in, come in. Are you hungry? Your room is down the hall on the left. Here, let me take this. How are you?"

The questions come hard and fast and I can't keep up. I just barely am able to grasp that I'm in New York, and the blue folder in my purse is burning against my side. Jess turns around as we walk down the hall and purses her lips together.

"Sorry. You must be exhausted. The twins and Owen are all asleep already. If you want to just pass out I'll get out of your hair."

"No," I say suddenly. Jess's eyebrows raise. I try to smile. "I mean, I'd rather spend a bit of time with you. If you don't mind." *I'm not ready to be alone yet,* is what I mean to say. Jess understands right away and she smiles.

"Here's your room. Drop your suitcase and come to the kitchen. I opened a bottle of wine just in case you wanted some when you got here," she says with a wink. I try to smile again but it feels like my face has forgotten how. Jess wraps me in a hug and squeezes me close.

"It'll be okay," she whispers.

I follow her to the kitchen and we sit at the little round table in the corner. She takes out two long-stemmed wine glasses and pours generous amounts of wine in each.

"Welcome to New York," she says with a grin as she raises her glass. We clink them together and I take a sip. The rich, bitter red wine fills my mouth and I sigh in satisfaction, feeling my shoulders relax right away.

"Thank you for having me," I finally say.

Jess shakes her head. "Don't be ridiculous. When you called I was ready to jump on a plane myself and go down to Lexington. You shouldn't be alone right now."

I try to respond but all of a sudden there's a lump in my throat. I lift the wine up to my lips and take the tiniest sip before putting it back down. My eyelids are prickling and my heart is thumping against my ribcage.

"How did this happen?" I whisper, finally lifting my tear-filled eyes up to Jess. "How did this happen?"

Jess reaches across the table to put her hand over mine. Her eyes are soft and caring and full of concern.

"It happened when that asshole broke his vows and showed his true colors," she responds.

"What did I do wrong?" I ask, shaking my head. "I was a good wife. We weren't even married three years. I cooked and cleaned and had a job and—"

"Stop," Jess says sternly. I glance up at her, surprised. "You did nothing wrong. Do you hear me? Absolutely nothing. Cheaters cheat, that's what they do. It doesn't matter who you are or what you do, it's him who did you wrong. It's him who did it to you and it's him who is the asshole. Not you. You are a fucking saint, if you ask me," Jess says as she takes a swig of wine. "I'd have keyed his car and burned all his things in the front yard."

I feel a hint of a smile breaking my lips. Jess glances at me and grins. Her smile fades and she shakes her head. "I thought you guys were the real deal. When I went to your wedding I thought I'd be visiting you when you were eighty with dozens of grandkids."

The tears prickle my eyes and I put my hand over my

forehead. I nod, because my voice is gone. Jess reaches over and rubs my back, cooing and making soft motherly noises.

"Come on, Sam. I know it's horrible now and it feels like it will always be horrible. But it won't. Look at the bright side, you have no kids. You have skills and drive and you can get a job anywhere. The house in Lexington is paid for, so you can sell your half to Ronnie and be done with that toxic town. You have *options*," she says. I finally lift my eyes up to her and she reaches across the table to hold my hand. "So many options. You hear me?"

"I hear you, but it still feels like my life is over," I say. "That sounds so pathetic," I add with a snort.

"No, it doesn't. It sounds completely reasonable."

Jess scoots her chair over and wraps her arms around me. I lay my head on her shoulder and finally let the tears flow. I cry into her shoulder as she holds me and rocks me back and forth. Finally, when the tears start to slow down I sit up. I take my wine and lift it to my lips to take a long drink.

"You're right," I say as I turn to Jess. A smile starts to form on her lips. "I have options."

"You do. And you can stay here as long as you want to. I mean it. As long as you want to."

I nod and smile. I don't respond because I don't trust my voice. The tears are prickling my eyes again, but this time they're tears of gratitude and love for my best friend.

"So," I clear my throat when the word comes out as a croak. "So it's the twins' birthday party tomorrow?"

Jess leans back in her chair and smiles. "Yes! Terrible twos," she laughs. "I thought the ones were terrible but apparently it gets worse!"

I laugh and shake my head. "I'm sure you'll manage."

"We will," she says with a smile, glancing down the hallway. A pang goes through my chest when I think of the partnership that Owen and Jess have. I thought I had that kind of love too—the kind of love that lasts decades. I was wrong.

"What's planned for the party?"

"We've got a clown coming!" Jess says with a laugh. "I didn't even know they still had clowns, but apparently you can hire them by the hour. They call themselves 'children's entertainers'."

I chuckle. "That's very glamorous."

"Very," Jess adds. "Anyways, this company is supposed to be really good. I just hope the kids like it and don't end up traumatized and scared of clowns for the rest of their lives."

"Scared of children's entertainers, you mean."

Jess laughs. "Yeah, right, sorry. Children's entertainers."

I lean back in my chair and my shoulders relax again. For the first time since I left Lexington, I feel my body begin to unwind. Jess talks and we laugh until the bottle of wine is empty, and then she wraps her arms around me once again. I sigh into the hug and then we just look at each other and nod.

"See you tomorrow," she says with a smile. "Sleep tight."

"You too," I answer. I walk to my bedroom and close the door, grateful that the wine is making my eyelids heavy. I might actually be able to sleep tonight.

3

DEAN

I CRAM all my gear into the car and swear. Of course I'm late. I had three alarms set and I still slept through them. You'd think I was a fourteen year old boy and not a grown man for the amount of sleep I need. I rush back up the elevator and jump into the clown costume.

Within a few minutes, I've got the costume on and I'm painting my face. The wide red smile and bright cheeks look ridiculous, but they help me get in character. I paint the black outline and big circles around my eyes. My hair gets gelled back and my wig slides on.

I take a deep breath and look at myself in the mirror. I'm ready. I slip my regular shoes on and carry my huge clown shoes down the elevator with the last of my props. I'm finally ready. I glance at my watch and shake my head. With a bit of luck I should get there only ten or fifteen minutes late.

Traffic seems to be on my side, and I drive through the streets more quickly than anticipated. I double check the address and park in front of a house. There are balloons swinging in the wind near the front door.

"This must be it," I say to myself. I slip my big shoes on and grab my bag of props. My hands are full but I'm able to carry everything in one trip. I slam the trunk closed and turn towards the front door.

The shoes are awkward to walk in, and I waddle my way up to the front door. I wish New York houses didn't have so many steps. I ring the doorbell and clear my throat, ready to put on my clown voice. The door swings open and a man appears on the other side.

"Clifford the clown, at your service," I say with a flourish, bowing with my arms outstretched. The man chuckles.

"Come on in, they're out back."

I follow him to the backyard and the sounds of children screaming and playing get louder. He slides the back door open and I step through. The kids turn to me immediately and start laughing. The show begins.

There's something special about performing for kids. The way their eyes shine and the way they laugh without a worry in the world makes me feel like I'm floating. Every time one of them laughs at something I do or falls for one of my pranks it feels like a mini jolt of energy to the heart.

These kids are no different. I spot the birthday twins right away: a boy and a girl. They're only two, but they're the life of the party. I give them party hats first, and then start handing them out to the other kids. I glance at the parents and hand out party hats to them as well.

As much as I didn't want to do this last night, I'm enjoying myself. I settle the kids into a semi circle in front of me and prepare them for the balloon animal bit of my performance. I pull out the air canister and blow up a long balloon. I start twisting it and tying it as the kids watch in awe.

When Pat first started teaching me to make these, it was

the most frustrating weeks of my life. It's definitely harder than it looks. It took me almost a year to get the hang of it, and I'm just now starting to feel confident.

I make the first balloon animal, a dog, and I hand it to the birthday girl.

"One for you," I say in my best Clifford the Clown voice. She giggles and waves it around and I grin. Next is a giraffe, and a monkey, and a shark. I make them one by one and hand them to the kids. By this time I'm really enjoying myself. I'm laughing along with them and I know I've got them in the palm of my hand. The adults are laughing at my jokes and I'm on a high.

I love my job.

I grab another balloon and stretch it long before starting to inflate it. Just as I start filling it with air, the sliding glass door opens and my jaw drops. She's got long brown hair that falls down well past her shoulders. Her nose has a sprinkling of freckles over them and her green eyes sparkle in the sun. She squints as she steps out, looking at me curiously. I let my eyes drop to her white tank top and tight jeans and my heart starts to race.

It's the balloon popping that brings me back to reality. It explodes in my hand and I jump. The kids jump and laugh and I pretend to fall over. They all laugh harder and I get up, pretending to struggle. I glance over at the woman. She's still standing by the door, leaning against the frame as if she's scared of getting too close to the party.

"You!" I call out to her. She stands up a bit straighter and looks over her shoulder and then back at me. "What's your favorite animal?" I ask.

She grins and shrugs.

"Come on," I say, taking a step closer. I glance back at the kids and they laugh. "You must have a favorite?"

Her smile widens and it almost knocks me over. I glance around and see all the parents coupled off. My eyes swing to the doorway and I wonder if her husband is inside.

"Elephant," she finally says.

"Elephant," I exclaim, making a trunk with my arm for the kids and pretending to swing it around. Their laughter reaches a peak. I pull out a balloon and get to work. When I hand her the elephant. She reaches out to accept it. Our fingers brush each other ever so gently. Even through the fabric of my white gloves I feel an electric current pass through my arm.

"Thank you," she says softly. She smiles at me and I feel my face relax. I stare at her for a few seconds before snapping back to myself. I'm Clifford the Clown right now. Dean Shelby doesn't exist. I turn back to the group of children, ready to make them laugh again. When I pull out another balloon, I can't resist turning back towards the woman. She's turning the elephant over in her hands and smiling. My heart grows in my chest.

Making a balloon elephant may be the best achievement of my life so far.

4

SAMANTHA

He made the elephant so fast I could hardly tell what he was doing, but then it appeared in his hands. I run my fingers over the big ears and long trunk and shake my head. Amazing. I glance back at the clown and watch as he waves his hands over the children and they all laugh and play along.

Jess wasn't wrong, he's very good. He glances over his shoulder and our eyes meet again. He smiles at me and sticks out his tongue before turning back to the group of kids. I can feel the pulse in my whole body and I glance back down at the balloon elephant, turning it around in my hands.

"Well, look at you," Jess says with a grin. "I haven't seen you smile since you got here."

I hold up the elephant. "Guess the clown is doing his job then, hey?"

Jess's grin widens. "I guess he is."

I choose to ignore the teasing in her voice. "I didn't expect him to be so..."

"...attractive?"

"No, young!" I answer quickly. "I didn't expect him to be

so young. I thought it would be a guy in his sixties for some reason."

Jess chuckles. "So did I. It's hard to tell what he looks like under that makeup, but based on that jawline I'd say he's quite a stud."

I roll my eyes. "Aren't you married?"

Jess grins at me. "I'm not looking for me, Sam," she says.

"Stop," I say. "I'm not even divorced yet. I'm not ready."

"Whatever you say," she replies. I glance back at the clown and try to imagine what his face would look like. He lifts his arms and the fabric of his costume pulls across his broad back. He's certainly muscular.

"Harper, Rosie!" Jess calls over. "Come over here and help me settle something."

"What are you doing," I whisper. She looks at me and grins again. The two women come closer and Jess nods to the clown.

"What do you think about Clifford? You think he's a hunk under all that makeup?"

Rosie and Harper turn towards the clown and suddenly all four of us are staring at him. Rosie tilts her head to the side and Harper squints.

"Definitely," Rosie says. "Certified stud." She turns back towards us and nods once, as if that's the official seal of approval. Jess laughs.

"I knew it. See, Sam? You should go for it!"

"Absolutely," Harper says. "The best way to get over someone is to get under someone else. I've never had sex with a clown before."

I start laughing and shake my head. "Stop, stop! I'm not sleeping with anyone!" I know they're only joking but I can't help the blush that starts to creep over my cheeks. Jess puts an arm around my shoulder and laughs.

"I'm only teasing. No harm in looking though. Come on, let's get you a drink."

She pulls me towards the kitchen and I steal one last glance towards Clifford the Clown. He's got the kids all lined up and somehow is getting them to jump and move exactly as he says. He definitely has a gift for working with children.

The four of us step inside and I listen as Harper, Rosie, and Jess talk about their kids. They laugh and joke about all the things that kids do, and I can't help but feel like the odd one out. Not only do I not have a child, but my marriage has been an absolute disaster.

The lightness that I felt when I was watching the clown perform starts to dissipate as thoughts about Ronnie creep in. I still remember the way he looked when I confronted him. He denied everything even though I had followed him to the restaurant and seen him kiss her. My whole world had crumbled around me.

He must have been cheating on me for months, maybe even longer. My throat tightens and I try to push the thoughts away when Jess appears beside me with a glass of chilled white wine.

"Here," she says with a whisper. "If I have one job today, it'll be to get you to drink and smile." She look up and towards the back door. "Where's Clifford? He was good at that."

I laugh and shake my head as Jess nudges my shoulder. The two other girls laugh. Just then, the laughter and children's screams outside get a little bit higher pitched. I hear an adult yell. The four of us look at each other and then rush outside.

It's carnage. I don't know how this happened in such a short amount of time. Clifford the clown is on the ground, holding his arm and writing around. The kids are running around in circles and Owen is trying to wrangle them. Matt, Jess's son, is swinging a plastic baseball bat wildly over and back. He knocks the clown's air canister and it falls with a loud clang.

Owen finally manages to grab Matt just as Jess starts herding the other children together. I jog over to the clown as he lies on the ground.

"You okay?" I say as he groans. His eyes slowly lift up to me and he blinks a few times.

"Yeah, yeah, I'm fine," he says and then groans as he tries to stand up. "My arm."

"What's wrong? What happened? We were only gone for a minute."

"That's all it takes," he says with a grimace. His regular voice is deep and gravelly. Despite all the clown makeup, something sparks between my legs. Even with all the clown makeup, I can see the way his eyes gleam when he smiles. "That one grabbed a bat and hit me," he says, nodding towards Matt. "I tripped over these stupid shoes and fell on my arm. I think it might be broken."

"Oh my goodness," I say softly. "Come on."

I help him to his feet and guide him to the kitchen. Soon, he's gone some ice on his arm and he's sighing. I grab a dish towel and wrap it around his arm in a makeshift sling.

"There," I say.

"Are you a nurse?" He asks as he admires my handiwork. I laugh.

"No, not a nurse. Just resourceful." I study his face for a minute before speaking again. "I'm Sam," I say after a pause.

"Clifford," he replies as his eyes spark again.

"Wait, is that your real name?" I ask as I try to hide the smile on my lips. He lets out a quick laugh and shakes his head.

"Dean Shelby," he says as he extends his good hand. "Nice to meet you."

The instant our hands touch it's like a current of electricity passes through my arm. His eyes are locked on mine and it feels like time stops.

He clears his throat. "Thank you," he says, motioning to the sling.. He shifts his weight and groans. "This is so painful."

"You're going to have to go to the hospital," Jess says as she comes back in through the door. I almost jump backwards. "I'm so sorry about this."

"It's fine," he says. He glances at me and winks. "Occupational hazards."

I can't help but laugh. "Dangerous job," I say.

"Very."

Jess glances at his arm and shakes her head. She puts her hands on her hips and sighs. "I'm so sorry, Clifford. So, so sorry. Can you drive? I'll call you a cab. I'm so sorry."

"I have a stick shift," he answers with a grimace. "So, no, I guess."

"I'll drive," I hear myself say. "I can drive stick and none of these kids are mine. I don't mind."

"Are you sure?" the clown says, knitting his eyebrows together. It gives his face an exaggerated sad look and I start laughing.

"She's sure," Jess responds with a raised eyebrow. "Here," she says, handing me some money. "For the cab back."

"Don't worry about it, Jess." I say with a smile.

"Then you take it," she says, thrusting the money into Clifford's sling. "For this whole mess. Call it a tip."

He just laughs and shakes his head. "It's really not necessary. It's fine, really. Kids get excited and it happens."

"Just take it," she says. "I feel so bad. I'm so sorry."

"Don't be." He grimaces again and I stand up a bit straighter.

"Come on," I say. "We should get you to the hospital sooner rather than later." I hook my arm around his shoulder and try to ignore the thrill that passes through me when our bodies touch. He groans as he stands up and then looks at the sling and nods approvingly.

"Let's go," he says, letting his eyes linger on mine for just a few moments. I blush and look away, not daring to look at him or Jess.

5
DEAN

The kid hit me right in the crotch and I doubled over immediately. These stupid clown shoes got in the way. I heard the crunch, and I felt the pain shoot through my arm. I'm pretty sure it's broken.

Usually I'd be mad right now, or at least annoyed, but as I slide into the passenger's seat of my car I feel a tingle of excitement. I watch as Sam circles the front of the car and climbs into the driver's seat.

"Thank you for doing this," I say as she slides the key into the ignition. She pauses and turns towards me with a serious expression on her face.

"Okay, one thing," she says as she holds up a finger. "Stop thanking me. It's getting old."

I fight the smile that starts to form on my lips and nod dutifully. "Of course. Anyone would go out of their way to help the children's entertainer and take time out of their day. Anyone would drive to the hospital when they could just call a cab. It's normal. Not worth thanking someone for that."

She glances at me sideways and starts the car. "You're going to have to navigate. I have no idea where I'm going."

I nod. "Take a left up here."

We drive in silence for a few minutes and I steal a glance over at Sam. The sun is just reaching its peak and it's shining through the window onto her face. It makes her hair look like a million different shades of brown. I watch as her hands glide over the steering wheel when she turns, and the way her eyes flick from the mirror back to the road.

She turns her head slightly towards me and I glance away.

"So," she starts, breaking the silence. "Do you actually refer to yourself as a children's entertainer?"

I glance over at her again and see her grinning as she watches the road. I make an exaggerated sigh. "It's an under-appreciated profession," I reply. "We take ourselves seriously."

"Do you have a guild? The children's entertainers guild?"

I fight the smile that starts forming on my lips. "We call it the Clown Club."

She laughs, and it's the first time I see her true smile. Her whole face lights up and the corners of her eyes crinkle as she laughs. Her shoulders move up and down and she shakes her head slightly. She glances over at me and grins.

"Sounds very exclusive."

"Oh, it is," I reply, leaning back in my seat. "Only the best of the best get to be in the Clown Club."

She laughs again, and something stirs in my chest. A smile drifts over my lips and I shift in my seat. My arm is throbbing, but somehow the pain seems dulled.

"Take the next exit over here, and the hospital is just on the right."

"Okay."

I watch as she grabs the steering wheel, loving how gracefully she moves. I wish it was me her hands were grabbing. She could run those delicate fingers over my skin and I could pull her body close to mine.

I try to shake the thoughts with a deep breath. She pulls into the hospital parking lot and parks the car.

"I'll grab a parking ticket, I'll be right back."

I nod and open my door before realizing I'm still in full costume. I sigh. I can't walk into the hospital like this. As much as I love my job, it does get a lot of attention. I have a change of clothes in the trunk, so I reach over and pop the trunk. I reach across my body and open the car door, wincing as I nudge my bad arm. I take a deep breath and swing my legs out. I had no idea how much I use my right arm until now.

I get out of the car as Sam comes back with a parking ticket. She puts it on the dash and looks at me with a questioning glance.

"I've got a change of clothes and some face wipes in here," I say, nodding to the trunk. She makes a small 'ah' sound and nods. I walk around to the trunk and start looking for the small black bag. I know it's in here, I always take it with me. I move some props and finally see it. It's pinned down by the air compressor and I try to pull it out. I wrench at it and pain shoots through my injured arm. I yelp, jumping back and wincing.

"What's wrong, are you okay?"

"I'm fine," I say, looking up to see Sam's concerned eyes looking at me. "Would you mind grabbing that bag from under there? It should have a tee-shirt and shorts in it."

I can't help staring as she bends over to reach the bag in

the trunk. Within a couple seconds she lifts it free and turns towards me. I look at the bag and she grins.

"Here," she says, unzipping it. She pulls out some face wipes and hands them to me. I sit down on the back of the car and she sits beside me. I struggle to open the package with one hand, and finally succeed in pulling out a face wipe. Sam grabs the package before it slides off my legs to the ground and I start wiping my face. I usually do this in front of a mirror, but I look at the wipe to see my progress. Sam laughs.

"I'll help you," she says. "You're just smearing it all over the place. You look like a horror movie villain right now."

"Gee, thanks," I say with a grin. She laughs and pulls out another wipe and starts at the top of my forehead, moving down. I close my eyes and enjoy her gentle touch as she wipes my face back and forth. Her other hand moves to my chin to steady my face. She wipes around my eyes and I groan in satisfaction.

"This is better than a spa treatment," I groan. Sam laughs. She pulls out another wipe and moves to my lips. I open my eyes and for an instant we stare at each other as she holds my face and wipes my lips with the cloth. She shakes her head slightly and looks back at my lips. My heart is beating harder than it was when I fell over and I can't stop staring at her face. She's beautiful.

Finally, she gathers the used wipes. "There," she says with a smile. "You look like a human again."

"Thanks," I say with a grin. "Is there a tee-shirt in there?"

"Here," she says and I take it from her with my good hand. I stand up and stuff it in the sling and start trying to unbutton my costume. The buttons are so big that it's hard to manage with one hand. The top button keeps sliding out of my grasp until finally I sigh in frustration. I look up to see Sam watching me with an amused smile on her face.

"Let me help you," she says softly. I gulp, trying to ignore the lump in my throat as I watch her hands get closer to me. One by one, she unbuttons the front of my clown costume to expose my chest. Her hands move slowly, and I run my eyes over her hands, her arms, her shoulders. Her breasts pull at the fabric of her shirt and her hair is still glimmering with a thousand different shades of brown. She's so close to me that I can smell the faint floral perfume she's wearing and my cock throbs between my legs. I shift my weight to try to hide it.

I watch her face as she tries to keep a steady expression, but I notice the blush that starts forming on her cheeks. When she reaches my bellybutton she stops and takes a step back.

"There," she says, turning away and glancing towards the hospital doors.

"Thanks," I respond, shimmying my good arm out of the long sleeve and working slowly to peel it off my bad arm. I wince and inhale sharply as I accidentally hit my arm. I reach behind my back to untangle the sling from my costume.

"Sam," I say softly. She swings her eyes back to me and I look at her, pleading with my eyes. "I'm sorry. Can you help me?"

6

SAMANTHA

My heart is bouncing against my ribcage and my cheeks are on fire. His chest is broad and muscular, and every time he moves I can see his muscles ripple under his skin. I can see the top of his abdominal muscles through the opening in his costume and my head is spinning.

I reach up and untangle his costume from the sling I made earlier, and slide the sleeve off his bad arm. He winces and grits his teeth as I try to move as gently as possible. I steal another look at his face and my heart thumps again. I could tell he was good-looking under his makeup, but I had no idea. His eyes are a piercing blue and his features are manly and defined. There's a hint of stubble across his jaw, and his lips are full and pink. I try to ignore the beating of my heart when I remember the look he gave me as I wiped off his makeup.

"There," I say as his arm finally comes free. I drop the sleeve and gasp as the costume drops towards his feet. He makes a noise and tries to grab the fabric as it falls. I look away, but not before I see his polka-dot boxer briefs. He tries to catch the costume before it falls and finally hikes it up above his hips. If I was blushing before, I'm definitely as red as a tomato now.

"Sorry," he says. I glance back at him and shake my head. The smile is starting to creep over my lips and I lift my eyes to his. My cheeks are still on fire and his eyes are sparkling.

"Do you always wear polka-dot boxer briefs or is that part of the Clown Club regulations?"

He laughs and his whole face brightens. He looks back at me and shakes his head. "That's just personal preference."

I chew my lip as I try to stop from smiling, hoping my cheeks aren't as red as they feel. I reach over to his tee-shirt and hold it up. "You need help with this?"

"Please," he says. "Look, I'm sorry. I really appreciate this."

"Its nothing. To be honest, it's better than being in a house with ten screaming children." *Way, way better than that.*

I bunch the shirt and help him put his head through the neck hole. He pulls his good arm through it and we both look at the sling and tee-shirt draped across his shoulder.

"This isn't going to work," I say. Dean laughs. He lifts his arm and I pull the shirt off him again. My chest just brushes against his and my fingers run over the skin of his arm. My heart thumps again and I shake my head to try to control myself. The flame between my legs is making my knees weak.

"Here," I say, sliding the sling off his arm. We move slowly, putting the shirt on over his injured arm first, and then moving to the rest of his body. My fingers brush the skin on his shoulder again and that familiar shot of electricity pulses through my arm. My whole body feels like it's a few degrees warmer than it was a few minutes ago.

Finally, his shirt is on and the sling is back on his arm. He grins and my whole body melts. I wish he'd stop being so handsome. I'd be able to function a lot better in this situation if I didn't feel like my panties were soaking through every time he looked at me.

"I think I can manage the shorts," he says. I nod

"I'll wait up here," I say, gesturing to the front of the car. I grab my purse from the front seat and lean against the hood. Within a couple minutes I hear the trunk closing and Dean appears beside me, looking nothing like he did an hour ago. In regular clothes, I can see how strong and athletic his body is. His shirt is stretched over his broad chest, and his shorts show off his defined legs. He grins at me.

"Hope that wasn't too traumatic for you."

"I'll live," I say with a smile. I nod to the hospital doors and we start walking side by side.

"You don't have to come in with me," he says. "I can manage from here."

"I'll wait until you're signed in and we know what's going on. If you need any paperwork or anything I can help you get it."

He moves his hand to my elbow and my heart thumps once again. I glance up at his face and see his features soften. He shakes his head slowly and opens his lips as if to speak. He closes them again and glances towards the hospital.

"Thank you," he finally says in a low voice. "It's not often that someone is so kind."

"I'm from a small town," I say with a smile, elbowing him gently on his good side. "I haven't been ruined by the big city yet."

"I don't think anything could ruin you," he growls before flicking his eyes in my direction. My core starts burning and the space between my legs starts to pulse. I don't know what to say, so I just blush and look away. We walk through the sliding glass doors and into the hospital

My heart is still beating hard by the time we walk up to the reception desk. The nurse talks and asks questions and soon we're being shepherded to a waiting area. I follow her lead, but all I can hear is a buzzing in my ear and all I can feel is the warmth of Dean's body next to mine. Finally we sit down in the waiting room's hard plastic chairs and I try to steady my heartbeat.

"Thank you, Sam, really," he says.

I laugh and hold up a finger. "What did I say in the car when we started driving here?"

"I know, I know," he says with a grin. "I just want you to know how much I appreciate your help."

All I can do is stare into those bright blue eyes. My voice is gone and there's a lump in my throat. I smile and Dean smiles back. He leans back in his chair and lets out all the air from his lungs..

"Well, if you insist on being here, you might as well tell me about yourself."

7
DEAN

I LOVE HEARING SAM LAUGH. It's like she's surprised whenever she does, and the surprise of her own laugh makes her laugh even more.

"Don't be so enthusiastic," she says with a grin. "You sure sound like you want to get to know me." I glance at her and smile. If only she knew how badly I want to get to know her.

"Is Sam short for Samantha?" I ask.

"Yeah. I'm from a small town in Virginia, just up here visiting my friend Jess. She's the one with the twins," she explains.

"She's the one with the dangerous son, you mean."

"That's the one," she laughs. "We've known each other for years and she offered to let me stay with her for a while."

I frown, wondering what she means. Did she need somewhere to stay or is she just visiting?

"So are you in town for long?"

"I'm not sure," she says, settling back into her seat. "I needed a change. I'll see how it goes."

"I know what you mean. I started doing this clown gig

about a year ago when I was just sick to the teeth of the corporate world. Change is good."

"Do you like it?"

"The clown job? Yeah, I love it. I get such a buzz of making the kids laugh."

She nods. "I worked with kids too. They have a way of making you feel like a superhero just for existing," she laughs. "So you like kids?"

"Love them. I thought I'd have a few of my own by now, but that doesn't seem to be in the cards for me."

"No?" she asks. I turn towards her and frown.

"How did this turn into my life's story? I thought we were talking about you. All I know is your name and where you're from."

She laughs and my heart jumps again. "Isn't that enough?"

I shake my head. "Not nearly enough."

She looks at me curiously and shrugs. "Well, if I told you I was getting a divorce, would you believe me?"

I frown and study her face. Her eyes are steady, staring at me and watching my reaction. I shake my head. "How is that possible? You seem so young."

She sighs. "I know. These things happen, I guess. I just have to sign the papers and then it's all over."

"Was it... was it mutual?" *Are you still hung up on him?*

"It was mutual in the sense that he wanted to fuck other people," she says. The venom in her voice surprises me, and all I do is nod in response. I understand completely. I wish I couldn't relate as well as I can. She shakes her head.

"I shouldn't be telling you this. We got so serious all of a sudden. I'm just in New York to try something new. I got in last night and so far it's been quite the experience," she says, sweeping her hand across the waiting room. I laugh.

"Don't wait here with me. It could be hours," I say. *I want you to wait with me though.* "Here, take my number. Let me take you out for dinner. As a thank you." She opens her mouth and I laugh. "If I can't say thank you at least let me show it."

Sam looks at me and tilts her head to the side. The corners of her lips lift up and she nods before pulling out her cell phone. "Sure," she says. "Why not."

I put my phone number in her phone and press 'call'. "Got it," I say, slipping my phone back in my pocket. We look at each other for a few moments and then Sam takes a deep breath. She sits back in her chair and turns to look at me. It's almost like we're stuck in a trance studying each other's faces. Finally she takes another breath and smiles.

"I should probably get back. Let me know how it goes here, and if you need anything. You going to be okay to get home?"

"Yeah, I'll be fine," I say. "You go enjoy the rest of your weekend. You've done more than enough for me today."

She smiles and stands up, slinging her purse over her shoulder. I stand up as well and we stand awkwardly in front of each other. It almost feels like I'm supposed to kiss her—or maybe that's just what I want to do. Finally she chuckles and puts her hand on my shoulder. She lifts her head up and places a soft kiss on my cheek. That sweet floral perfume hits my nostrils again and I inhale deeply, letting my free arm graze against her side. She pulls away and smiles at me.

"I'll see you later," she says. "Nice to meet you."

"Nice to meet you too," I say. My heart pulls at me as I watch her walk away. It's not until she turns the corner and is out of view that I slump back down in my chair. Somehow the room feels colder and darker now, and the chair seems harder than it was five minutes ago. I look at the place where Sam disappeared around the corner and shake my head. I wasn't expecting to meet a woman like that today.

8

SAMANTHA

My head is spinning when I walk back out the sliding glass doors. I glance over at the nearby taxi rank and shake my head. Might as well take the subway back to Jess's place and explore this city a little bit. I'm in no rush to get back to the house anyways.

I check my phone for directions and head down the street, following the little blue line on the screen. I slip my phone back in my pocket and sigh. My heart feels lighter than it has in days. I haven't thought of Ronnie in hours.

Ronnie.

As soon as his name pops into my mind, a chill goes down my spine. The hurt is still raw. If I think of him too long, the heartache starts to sink into my bones. Every time I think of him it's like rubbing salt on the wound. It stings. My face falls and my brows knit together as I keep walking towards the subway station.

Should I be going out on a date with a guy I just met? I'm not even divorced yet! That blue folder is still laying on top of the dresser in my room where I left it last night. I square my shoulders. I feel more ready to sign them than I did yesterday. If I'm honest, I feel more ready to sign those papers now than I did a couple hours ago.

Dean's body paints itself in my mind's eye. I remember the way his skin felt when my fingertips brushed against his shoulder, and the way his whole body rippled with muscles. Every time he looked at me I felt like blushing, and every time he spoke it sent vibrations through my chest.

I make it to the subway steps and head down. For a few minutes, I think about nothing except where I'm going and which train to get on. As soon as the subway gets to the platform and I slide inside, I find a seat and think of Dean again.

My heart hasn't beat that hard in ages. I think of his little polka-dot boxer briefs and the way his cock was outlined. Is it just me or was he a little bit hard? My cheeks start to blush at the thought of it. I shake my head to dispel the thoughts. Of course he wasn't hard. That's a bit presumptuous of me to think that I could turn him on by just being next to him.

I'm just horny and alone and heartbroken and he's the first man that's given me any attention since Ronnie, that's all.

Still, when I think about the look that Dean gave me when I was wiping his face, somehow it feels like a little bit more than passing flirtation.

Before I know it, the subway is sliding into the station and I jump up to get off. I make my way up the stairs and spin around at the top to get my bearings. I glance at my phone and nod slowly, heading off in the direction of Jess's house.

I don't know what to think. I let my feet take me back to her house and climb the steps slowly. I slip in the front door, trying not to make too much noise. Footsteps come down the hallway and Jess appears.

"Sam! I was starting to wonder where you were. Did you

make it to the hospital okay? How much was the cab? Is Clifford okay?"

It takes me a second to realize she means Dean. I nod. "I took the subway back. It was fine," I say. *It was great, actually.* "I left before they saw him but it's probably broken."

"Oh gosh," Jess says, shaking her head. "I'm going to have to call the company and send a card. Matt is in his room. Apparently he hit him right in the crotch with the baseball bat, Owen saw everything."

I grin. "Disaster."

"Tell me about it," Jess says over her shoulder as we walk back towards the kitchen. "I have some spaghetti made if you want any?"

"Sounds great." I grab a plate and help myself to some food as Jess putters around the kitchen. I watch her and laugh. "I never knew you'd be the domestic type. You used to be the party animal!"

"Well, twins will do that to you," she says with a wry smile. "I hardly have a minute to myself."

"Sit and eat with me," I say. Jess glances at me and smiles.

"Okay," she nods. When we're both sitting down she looks at me and shakes her head. "You're in a very good mood. What happened?"

"Nothing," I say, spinning my fork to get a big bite of pasta. "I might have a date though, so don't worry about the apology card."

Jess's jaw drops and she lets out a laugh. "What!"

I shrug. "I don't know how it happened. He's really nice! And funny."

"Clifford the Clown is taking you out," she laughs. "Good for you," Jess says with a satisfied nod. "That's exactly what you should be doing."

There's a pang in my chest but I ignore it. "You should see him without that costume on," I say with a smile. "He looks even better."

"Jesus, Sam, you didn't...?"

"No! God, no. He just changed out of his costume before going to the hospital." For some reason I don't want to tell her about helping him change. I don't want to tell her about wiping his face or seeing his bare chest and boxer briefs. I want those moments to stay locked away inside me. Saying them out loud feels like it would somehow cheapen them.

"Right," Jess says, shaking her head. "I was thinking that would be out of character for you."

"Also, he has a broken arm," I say with a laugh. A twin appears in the doorway completely naked, with water trailing all behind her. Jess jumps up and wraps Michelle in her arms, carrying her back down the hallway. I shake my head and finish my food in silence before washing my dishes and heading to my room.

I close the door and lean against it, grateful for a bit of quiet. The blue folder is still sitting on top of the dresser, exactly where I left it last night. I narrow my eyes and walk towards it. I fling the folder open and look at the dozen little yellow tabs on all the sheets, all waiting for my signature.

There's a pen in my purse somewhere, so I rummage around until I find it. I take it out, pulling the cap off in a quick movement. I flick through the pages, signing and initialing where I'm supposed to. My heart is thumping and by the time I get to the last page, my eyes are starting to get blurry. I take the yellow envelope at the back of the files and stuff the papers inside. It's already stamped and addressed, so I lick the flap and seal it shut. I can't see anything from the tears in my eyes, so I sit down on my bed. The pen drops to the floor and I put my head in my hands as I let the tears flow from my eyes.

I cry for a few minutes before sniffling and wiping my face. I sit up a bit straighter and square my shoulders, glancing at the folder. With a deep breath, I get up and wipe the last tear away from my eye.

It's done. The papers are signed, and now they just need to be dropped in a mailbox.

I'm as good as divorced.

9

DEAN

"There you go," the nurse says as she smooths my shirt back down over my shoulder. "All done. Just stop by reception on your way out and you're free to go!"

"Thanks," I say absent-mindedly. Ever since Sam left the hospital, the day has dragged on endlessly.

The cast is bright white and heavy on my arm. They've given me a real sling, handing the old tea towel back to me. I glance at the rag and wonder if I should give it back to Sam or not. I stuff it in my pocket and head towards the hospital reception.

Before I get there, my phone starts vibrating in my pocket. My heart jumps and I wonder if Sam is calling me already. I pull out my phone from my pocket and duck over to an empty waiting room.

Of course she isn't calling me.

"Mother," I say as I answer the phone.

"Dean. How are you?"

"I'm fine," I say as I glance down at my cast. "I'm okay."

"Good. I thought about our conversation yesterday and I wanted to apologize." *Apologize? My mother is apologizing?*

"Okay..." I answer slowly.

"Are you free for dinner tonight? We've had the chef prepare a roast with all the trimmings. Your favorite."

"Tonight? Can we do another night, during the week maybe?" I hate how whiney I sound. My mother always brings out the worst in me.

"No, honey, your father will be out of town. Do you have plans tonight?"

I consider lying, but finally sigh and tell her the truth. "No, no plans. What time do you want me to come over?"

"Come over around seven. See you then, darling."

The phone clicks and I shake my head. I take a deep breath and start walking over towards the reception desk. When the phone rang in my pocket I thought I might have a date tonight. Instead I'm going to have to listen to my parents drone on and on and on. Maybe they'll tell me I ruined their political aspirations, or maybe they'll tell me they want grandkids. I can pretty much guarantee that whatever they want to tell me, I don't want to hear it.

I can't help it that Victoria turned out to be an awful excuse for a human. By the sounds of it, Sam has gone through something similar.

I still remember the look on Victoria's face when I walked into the bedroom. It was a mix of shock and guilt and then complete denial. How can you deny what's happening when you're completely naked with another man?!

The sliding glass door open and I'm hit with a wall of fresh air to cool me down. I take a deep breath and shake my head. I can't keep dwelling on the past. I'll just have to find a way to move on from Victoria, and I'll have to convince my parents to do the same.

Even as I think it now, the sting of her betrayal doesn't feel so harsh. My thoughts drift to Sam as I walk towards my car. She's so sharp, she always has a witty answer for me. I love the way she laughs and the way her whole body flows whenever she moves.

It's not until I get to my car that I remember I don't have two working arms. If anything, the cast has made it worse. I sigh and pull out my phone.

"Jacob, what's up," I say as my best friend picks up the phone.

"Dean, bro! How have you been? I haven't seen you in weeks!"

"We went out together two weekends ago," I remind him as I shake my head. I lean back against my car and watch the traffic go by. Jacob laughs.

"Yeah, whatever. It feels like weeks. What's up? We going out tonight?"

"I have dinner at my parent's. Maybe after, I think I'm going to need a drink." Jacob laughs and I continue. "Listen, buddy, can you do me a favor? I'm at the hospital, I broke my arm on a job this morning. Can I send an Uber to you and you can drive me back to my place?"

"No problem, man. I'm just at home so send it here."

"Thanks." I hang up the phone and tap on the screen a few times before heading back towards the hospital. I might as well wait in the air conditioning. I slump in the nearest chair and pull out my phone. I flick through the same social media apps that I've been flicking through since Sam left the hospital. Finally, I pull up my messages. I find Sam's number and start typing.

Dean: Did you make it home okay?

The minutes tick by and I check my phone a few times before sighing and putting it down. I have that excitement in the pit of my stomach that a fourteen year old boy gets when he's going on his first date. Finally, my phone buzzes and I pick it up. Sam's name is on the screen with the words 'photo message'. My heart starts thumping as I wonder what she could have sent me. My fingers are almost trembling as I unlock my phone and click the notification.

I frown when I see a picture of a yellow legal envelope next to a USPS mailbox. That's not exactly what I was expecting. The three little dots under the photo tell me she's typing an answer.

Sam: I'm officially a divorcee, I'm sending off the papers now. Feels like I should celebrate somehow.

I grin and start typing.

Dean: Did meeting me push you over the edge? I didn't know I'd had that effect on you.

I press send and immediately see the three little dots appear. I love that she isn't playing games and waiting to message me back. I laugh when her message appears.

Sam: 🙄

I shake my head. Even over text message she can make me laugh.

Dean: Celebrate with me tonight. I'm having dinner at my parent's house but I can meet you for a bit of champers after 🥂

Sam: Sounds good xx text me later

I slip my phone in my pocket just as I see Jacob walking through the front doors. He opens his arms out wide and shakes his head.

"Who's the punk who did this to you! I'll beat him up!"

I laugh. "A two year old."

"Where does he live, I'll head there now. No one beats up my friends," he says, puffing up his chest. I laugh and get up off the chair and clap him on the back.

"I can't believe you're still doing the clown thing," he says as he shakes his head. "I thought for sure you'd get bored of that."

"I wasn't kidding when I said I wanted to give back. Working at my father's investment firm isn't exactly fulfilling."

"Fulfillment is bullshit," he says with a laugh. "Come on, let's go. What time is dinner at your parent's place? I was thinking we could check out that new club on 4th."

"Actually, I don't think I can go out with you. I may have a date tonight."

"You're blowing me off for a chick?!" He says as he stops walking and puts a hand to his heart. "I'm hurt, Dean. You've changed."

I chuckle. "Sorry, man."

"Who is she," he grins. He glances back. "One of the nurses?"

I shake my head.

"One of the moms?!" He asks with his eyes wide.

I laugh. "No. One of the mom's friends. She drove me to the hospital."

"Dude!" Jacob says with an approving nod. "Well done!"

I laugh and shake my head. I want to tell him it's not like that. I don't want it to be a one night stand or a fling. I actually want to get to know this girl. I haven't felt that way since before I got engaged to Victoria. I nod towards the exit.

"Come on," I grin. "Let's go."

"Yeah you've got a busy night ahead," he says as he elbows

me right in the arm. Pain shoots through my side and I wince, grabbing the cast and doubling over.

"Shit, sorry Dean, I forgot," he says as he puts a hand on my back. I just laugh and shake my head.

"Typical," I say as I straighten up. I look at him with a grin as I shake my head. "Typical."

Jacob shrugs and grins. "At least you'll get some major sympathy points with this chick."

"Let's go," I say. Jacob laughs and the two of us head out towards my car.

10

SAMANTHA

I STARE at the screen and my heart starts thumping. Is this a date? I haven't been out on a date with a man in years. I turn away from the mailbox and walk back down the street towards the house. I find Jess in the living room with the twins. They're playing together on the ground and she's folding laundry with Owen.

"So, I think I might have a date," I say as I pick up some clothes and start helping them. Jess drops her hands and stares at me.

"What?! How?! Is it the clown?"

Owen looks up and frowns. "The clown?"

I grin. "Children's entertainer, thank you very much." They both laugh and I shrug. "He texted me to make sure I made it home okay and then invited me out for a drink. Is that a date? Or is it just, I don't know, being polite?"

Owen laughs. "It's a date. He texted to make sure you made it home okay? What did you guys do at the hospital??"

My thoughts flick back to the parking lot, when our bodies were inches away from each other and I could feel the heat of his skin under my fingers. I can feel myself blushing already and I shake my head, staring at the pile of laundry as I fold with them.

"We just talked," I say. "So it's a date?"

They both chuckle. "It's a date," Jess says. "What time are you meeting him?"

"I'm not sure yet. He said he was having dinner at his parent's house."

"Cute," Owen says. "Family man. I like that."

Jess rolls her eyes and chuckles. "Don't listen to him. Let's finish this and I'll help you choose an outfit."

I smile and nod. Jess winks at me and in no time we have the laundry folded and are heading back to my room to check out my clothes.

"So I think you should go with something sexy but understated, you know? Like casual but still a bit saucy." Jess looks over at me and smiles. "I'm so glad you're doing this!"

I try to smile. "I'm nervous, Jess. I haven't been on a date in so long."

She puts her arm around me and squeezes me into her. She smells like fresh laundry and babies. "Don't worry. It doesn't have to mean anything, and he doesn't have to be 'the one' or whatever. You're just going out and having a drink and having fun."

I nod and try to blink back the tears. She wraps both arms around me and hugs me tightly. My voice is muffled in her shoulder when I speak.

"I signed the papers and sent them," I blurt out.

Jess pulls away. "Is that where you went when you said you were going for a walk?" Her eyes are soft and full of concern. I nod and she sighs. "Oh, Sam," she say softly. "I'm sorry."

I take a deep breath and shake my head. "It's a good thing. It had to be done. It just feels so... final."

"Well that asshole doesn't deserve another second of your thoughts, you hear me?" She puts her hands on my shoulders and looks me straight in the eye. "Not another second. You go out and have a drink and flirt and maybe even kiss. And who knows? You might get lucky!"

My heart thumps in my chest and I shake my head. "I don't know. I don't know if I should be doing this. It feels like it's too soon."

Jess scoffs. "People love to judge others for moving on too soon. I say the quicker the better. Ronnie didn't give you the respect to be faithful during your marriage, and now you're a free woman. You don't need to jump into bed with anyone! All I'm saying is if another man wants to give you attention and a bit of affection, then enjoy every single second of it."

I nod and wipe my cheeks. A few tears have fallen out of my eyes and I quickly brush them away. Jess pulls me in for another hug and then takes a step back and claps her hands together.

"Okay. We only have a few hours. What are you wearing? I'm thinking tight jeans and a sexy tank top. Maybe with a cropped blazer and some good accessories? We can blow dry your hair and give you a nice smokey eye. I'm thinking soft pink lips, nothing too bold. You know, something... kissable."

I can't help but laugh. My throat still feels tight and my laugh comes out as a gurgle, but I nod my head and sniff my nose.

"Sounds good. How about this top?" I say as I pull out a black camisole with a lacy trim. Jess nods.

"Perfect."

I smile and take a deep breath. She's right. A date is just a date, and a drink is just a drink. I'm divorced now, and I'm allowed to go out and enjoy myself. I'm not doing myself any favors by wallowing by myself at home. If a sexy, funny man who happens to be very caring and loves kids wants to take me out for a drink, then who am I to refuse? I should go out and enjoy myself.

Jess and I go through my wardrobe and my accessories. Pretty soon the nervousness dissipates and all that's left is excitement.

11

DEAN

"Hello, mother," I say as she opens the front door.

"Dean, darling. When are you going to stop calling me that! It sounds so formal." *Probably never.* Her hands fly up to her mouth and she motions to my arm. "What happened!"

"Occupational hazard," I say with a grin. "Just got the cast on today."

"When did this happen. We can get Dr. Long to look at it this evening!"

"Mother, I've been to the hospital already. It's broken in two places but they set it and put a cast on it. It's fine, just a bit sore."

She makes a noise and I smile as she ushers me inside. I can smell the roast already, and I take a deep breath in. My mother's new cook came highly recommended, and I can already see why.

We walk through the grand foyer and into the living room. They've hired a new decorator. The overstuffed sofas and Persian rugs of my youth have been replaced with an ultra-sleek, modern-looking decor. I whistle.

"Big change!"

My mother waves her hand lazily. "Oh, you know. It was time for something fresh. Change is always good."

My eyebrows shoot towards my hairline as I nod. "I'll agree with you there, change is definitely good." My thoughts drift to Sam. I can still see her as she drove, when the sun was shining on her face making it look like she had a halo. Change is definitely good.

My mother floats towards the bar and pours us both a drink. I take the glass of whiskey and sniff, already knowing it'll be the best of the best. She sits down beside me as my father enters the room.

"Dean!" He exclaims in his big booming voice. He walks in with his arms outstretched, dominating the whole room. He is always the centre of attention. "How is my favorite son doing today. I'm glad you could make it. What's this!"

He points to my cast and I'm already tired of explaining myself. I'm guessing it'll be happening a lot these days.

I tell them both about the twins's birthday party this morning, but I leave out the part where Sam drove me to the hospital. It feels wrong to tell them about it. I want to keep her locked away far away from them, far from where they can taint her.

"Will you be able to come in to work on Monday?" My father asks, eyeing my cast. I chuckle and shake my head. The only thing he's ever been concerned with is work.

"Yeah, I'll be fine. Might be a bit slower when I type but the rest of me is still fully functional."

"Good. Well! We have a surprise for you and it sounds like it's just arriving!" He says as the doorbell rings. It's not a regular doorbell, it sounds like chimes ringing through the entire mansion. I raise my eyebrows and look towards the living room entrance. My mother jumps up out of her seat and smooths her hands over her pants. I hear the clack-clack-clack of heels walking down the hardwood floors. Alarm bells start ringing in my head.

I know that walk.

I stand up just as Victoria turns the corner. Her eyes float up to mine and my veins turn to ice. My stomach drops and all I can do is stare at her. My mother glides over to her, crooning and saying things I can't quite understand. All I can do is stare at the woman who broke my heart.

She's perfectly made up, as usual. Her jet black hair is pulled into a low bun, and her clothes look expensive and perfectly tailored. Her purse hangs lazily off her forearm. She greets my mother with a kiss on either cheek and turns her eyes to me. A chill runs down my spine and I'm still frozen in place.

"Well don't just stand there, Dean, come and say hello!" My mother's voice draws me out of my stupor. I swing my eyes to her and frown.

"What is she doing here?"

"Dean," she titters nervously, "don't be so rude."

"I'll be as rude as I fucking want," I snap. "What is she doing here?"

"We invited her, son," my father says as he puts his hand on my shoulder. "Victoria has been speaking to us and she says she's ready to forgive you for leaving her like you did."

"Wait, what? *She's* ready to forgive *me*?" Am I Alice? Is this Wonderland? Is everything backwards? What is going on!

My mother walks over to me, guiding Victoria closer. With every clack of her heels on the ground it's like a dagger pierces my heart. She gets close enough that I can smell that perfume she always wears—the one I grew to hate. I shake my head.

"Is this why you had me over for dinner? I should have known," I say with a scoff. "It's never just about having dinner with you two. There's always an ulterior motive and it's always self-serving. Unbe-fucking-lievable," I say, side-stepping and heading for the exit.

"Dean!" my mother shouts. I stop in my tracks and spin around. She's breathing heavily, her chest heaving up and down. "It would be a good idea for you to reconsider your attitude." *Is that a threat?* "Victoria has been gracious enough to come over and hear you out, the least you can do is spend a bit of time with her."

"She was gracious enough to come alone, I see. Or is your lover waiting for you in the car?" My words come out like venom and Victoria bristles. Finally, she speaks.

"Dean, baby, I just came over to try to fix things up. Your mother has been inconsolable, you know how much is riding on our wedding. I told you I was sorry." Her voice is sickly sweet and she sways her hips as she walks towards me. Her heels bang on the ground and I resist the urge to shiver. I take a step back as she raises her hand to touch my arm.

"Enjoy your roast," I say before spinning on my heels and walking out. I make my way to the black Bentley and slide inside. I remember when my parents bought this car for me, how happy I was. Now it's nothing but a reminder of their power over me.

I sigh and bang my hand on the steering wheel with my good hand. "Fuck!" I yell. My heart is thumping and I can't think straight. She's been talking to my parents? They're not going to let this go. It sounded like my mother was threatening me! I take a deep breath and start the car.

This is an automatic, at least, so I can drive myself around even with an injured arm. The car rumbles to life silently, and I put it into gear. It's a gorgeous car, and it drives like a dream, but it's too flashy for me. I don't like taking it anywhere because it gets too many looks. When I drive out of my parent's gate, I let out a sigh.

So much for dinner.

I pull over on the side of the road and shift my weight to get my phone out of my pocket.

Dean: Dinner ended a bit early. How about that drink? Where are you?

I lean back in my seat and take a deep breath. The best thing I can do to get Victoria and my parents out of my mind is to see Sam. Even if she wasn't attractive and smart and sexy, at least she's *normal*.

12

SAMANTHA

JESS GIVES me a thumbs up as I get up to leave. I laugh and roll my eyes.

"I'll see you in a few hours," I say.

"Or not," she replies with a wink. I shake my head and open the door. When I look up, my jaw drops immediately. In front of the house is a gleaming black Bentley. At least, I think it's a Bentley. I've never seen one in real life before.

Dean is leaning against the passenger's side door. He's wearing a proper sling now, and is dressed in dark denim jeans and a dark blue button-down shirt. He smiles when I walk out and my heart does a backflip. He looks really, really good.

I walk down the steps and try to ignore the beating of my heart. My hands are shaking and I hope that my palms aren't sweaty. I don't know if I can trust my voice right now. I walk towards him and he leans in to kiss my cheek. I inhale his musky smell and brush my lips against his cheek. His stubble tickles my skin and I smile as I pull away.

"You look amazing," he says in a low voice.

"Oh, this old thing," I say with a wave, gesturing at the outfit that Jess and I carefully crafted over the past two hours. I'm wearing my favorite jeans and that black camisole, and Jess helped me fix my hair so it falls around my face in loose waves. I'm wearing more makeup than I normally would, but it's just enough to make me feel like a bombshell.

Dean laughs and pulls the car door open.

I whistle. "I thought you couldn't drive. This is quite the upgrade! Weren't you driving a Honda before?"

He shrugs. "This is my automatic."

"Right, of course," I say as I give him a thumbs up. "My automatic Bentley is just parked out back." He laughs and I shake my head. "Who are you?"

His lips curl upwards and he gestures towards the open car door. "Tonight, I'm your chauffeur, your date, your tour guide, your beau, anything you want me to be."

"My beau! That's a bit presumptuous, don't you think?"

He just winks at me and closes the door when I swing my legs inside. It's incredibly spacious, and I sink into the luxurious leather seats. I watch as he walks around the front and take a second to run my fingers along the smooth polished wood panelling. I've never been in a car like this.

Dean slides into the driver's seat and turns to me with a smile.

"What do you say we go to a favorite spot of mine?"

"Lead the way," I say with a smile. "I don't know the city at all. You're my tour guide, aren't you?"

He chuckles and starts the car. We drive through the streets and I can't believe how quiet the car is. Dean turns on the radio for a bit of low background music. I can see heads turning as we drive by, and I wonder if they'd ever guess that a small town girl from Virginia is in here. I glance over at Dean.

"So, I'm guessing either 'children's entertainer' isn't your main occupation, or you have some dark side that I won't be allowed to hear about. Which one is it?"

Dean laughs. He glances over at me and winks before turning back towards the road. "My father owns an investment banking firm. This car was a present from my parents."

"Are you close? With your parents, I mean."

Dean's eyebrows draw together slightly and he shrugs. He leans back in his seat and adjusts the sling before answering. "Depends what you mean by close."

"I mean like you spend a lot of time with them and they're important to you."

"Well I work with my father, so I spend a lot of time with him by definition," he says with a laugh. "We're here."

We pull up to a building and I see a small sign for a bar. Dean gets out of the car and comes around to open the door for me.

"You only have one good arm, you shouldn't be doing that for me," I say with a smile. He shrugs and leans me towards the building. His hand sweeps down my spine to rest in the small of my back and a shiver of excitement runs through me. He's so close to me I can almost hear his heartbeat.

He can probably hear mine, it feels like my heart is bouncing violently against my chest. We step down the stairs together and I grab the door at the bottom.

"I'll get this one," I say with a grin. He smiles at me and we step through to a dark jazz bar. I swing my eyes around the room to see a three-piece band playing on a small stage in the corner. The whole room is dimly lit with exposed brick walls on all side.. The bar is black and shiny, and we head over to sit on two stools near the end. I look around at the plush booths and rich wood wainscoting and I smile.

"This place is cool!"

"I know," he says, glancing towards the band. "I love coming here. It's like a little hideaway."

He motions to the bartender and orders a bottle of champagne. Once the glasses are in front of us he hands me one and lifts his own towards me.

"To new beginnings," he says. "And congratulations on your divorce."

I grin. "To new beginnings."

We drink together, staring at each other until the last moment when we tip our glasses back. The bubbles explode on my tongue and I put my glass down. I smile. Jess is right. I can enjoy myself tonight, and enjoy his company. This doesn't have to be anything more than a bit of flirtation and a bit of fun.

13

DEAN

I'M TRYING NOT to stare at the way her jeans are hugging every curve, or the way the lace on her chest is giving me just a hint of cleavage. I knew she was good-looking before, but seeing her dressed like this is making my cock throb.

All the stress of my parent's house dissipated the moment she walked out of her house. I'm a bit embarrassed to be driving her around in the Bentley, but what can I do. It's where I come from, and I can't hide it forever.

Sam looks at me curiously and shakes her head.

"You're a mystery," she says with a smile. "I thought you were just a struggling artist before, and now I find out you're actually an investment banker. How did the clown thing come up?"

"It sounds cliche, but I just wanted to give back. I don't know if you've ever worked in the financial sector, but it's completely ruthless. I felt myself getting out of touch. I met Pat, the guy who owns the clown business, and I fell in love with it."

I glance at her to try to gauge her reaction. It feels good to tell her these things. She smiles at me and I know that she gets it. Most people that are around me—my parents, friends, colleagues—they all dismiss the clown job as a phase. It doesn't feel like a phase though, it feels like the most important thing I've ever done. Sam nods her head and I feel like she understands that right away.

I take a sip of champagne and then turn my head towards her. "How about you? What do you do?"

Sam smiles and a thrill goes through my chest. "I actually work with kids as well, in non-profit. In Virginia I ran an after-school program for underprivileged kids, but now I'm not sure what to do. I'm just taking some time off and trying to come to terms with the fact that I'm divorced." She shakes her head and stares off towards the band. "It still sounds so weird to say it."

"I'm sorry," I say. "I know I was saying we're celebrating but I can't imagine how hard it is for you."

Sam's eyes flick back to mine and she smiles sadly. "It's fine. It's for the best."

"I went through something similar," I find myself saying. "I thought I was getting married, I thought she was 'the one', whatever that means."

Sam laughs. "I love that. 'The one'. Such bullshit."

"Completely," I say. Our eyes meet again and she smiles before taking a sip of champagne. I watch the way her lips curl on the glass , and the way she holds the stem delicately in her fingers. I take a sip of my own drink and then nod towards the band.

"You want to dance?"

"Sure," she says with a shy smile. My chest immediately tightens and I stand up, holding my hand towards her. She slips her fingers into mine and it feels like an electric current running through me. If I had ice in my veins at my parent's house, it's completely gone. Now it feels like my whole body is on fire.

We walk out to the small square dance floor in front of the band, and I slide her fingers onto my shoulder. She places her other hand on my shoulder and stands a bit away from me.

"Is this okay? I'm not hurting you?" she asks, glancing at my arm.

I shake my head. "It's perfect. I wish this thing wasn't in the way," I laugh. I slide my hand down to her waist and she inches closer. Her head comes a bit closer to mine and we sway slowly to the music. I inhale and close my eyes, trying to ignore the thumping of my heart. I run my fingers a little bit further behind her waist until my fingertips are brushing the hem of her jeans. I can feel the silky fabric of her shirt and the lace trim and all I want to do is slide my hand under her shirt to feel her skin.

She inches a bit closer and rests her head on my good shoulder. Her arms are draped around my neck and I wrap my good arm further around her. We move together slowly, swaying back and forth and inching closer to each other.

It feels like heaven. My whole body is vibrating and I can feel the heat of her skin so close to mine. Her hair smells so fresh. She's trailing her fingers over and back on the nape of my neck, sending shivers down my spine. My cock is throbbing between my legs and I close my eyes to try to control myself. All I want to do is pull her closer and crush my lips against hers. I just want to take her home and rip all these clothes off her and tangle my fingers into her hair before kissing her harder than I've kissed anyone before. I want to taste her and touch her and feel every curve of her body under my fingers.

She moves her hands from the nape of my neck across my shoulders and lifts her head. She looks at me with those dark green eyes of hers and a shiver runs through my body. Her lips start to curl up into a shy smile and she tilts her head to the side.

"Thank you for taking me out tonight," she says softly. "It's been a really nice day." She glances at my arm and then shakes her head. "I mean, probably not that nice for you. But considering those papers I signed and how awful I felt yesterday. I don't know. I'm rambling. It's just nice." Her eyes lift back up to mine and I smile.

"My day has been perfect," I respond. "I wish I broke my arm all the time if it meant I got to spend this much time with a beautiful woman like you."

Her smile widens and she brings her forehead back to my shoulder. I pull her in a bit closer and she wraps her arms around my neck again. We sway to the music, and I shut my eyes and enjoy her closeness.

14

SAMANTHA

As we move back and forth in each other's arms, I rest my head against his shoulder. He has one arm around me and I try not to touch his injured side. He cradles me in his arm and we move back and forth. My mind is completely quiet.

I don't remember the last time I felt so peaceful. From the moment I started suspecting that Ronnie wasn't faithful to the moment I dropped those papers in the mailbox, my mind has been a hurricane of thought and emotion. I've hardly been able to finish a thought before three other thoughts start knocking on my brain.

But now, as the sounds of the band surround us and we dance, my mind is quiet. I don't think of anything except how good it feels to have his arm around me, and how his cologne reminds me of a forest after the rain. His hand moves gently back and forth over the small of my back, and he presses his fingers into me to pull me closer. My body feels like a puppet, and every little movement he makes I respond to right away.

For the first time in months, I just let myself go. I close my eyes and rest my head on his shoulder. My breath slows down and all I do is *exist*. For these few minutes with Dean, I'm perfectly content, perfectly at ease, perfectly safe.

All too soon, the band stops an we separate. I turn to the band and clap while Dean smacks is good hand against his thigh. I look at him and smile, and I see a spark in his eye when he smiles back. He motions back to our seats.

I settle in beside him and our thighs come to touch. He brings his uninjured hand down to rest on my knee and stares into my eyes.

"So have you decided how long you're going to stay in New York?" His question comes out softly, almost hesitantly.

I turn to my glass of champagne and run my fingers up and down the stem. I take a deep breath and shrug before swinging my eyes back to him.

"I'm not sure," I finally say. "I like it here. I was thinking I might stay."

Did I just see his face brighten? It's hard to tell in this light. His fingers press ever so slightly into my thigh and he nods.

"I think you should," he says softly, barely above a whisper. His voice is like a growl that sends vibrations through my chest every time he speaks. I can feel myself blushing, and something sparks between my thighs. I swallow and turn back to my glass of champagne, trying to ignore the lump in my throat. Dean does the same, and the second his hand leaves my thigh I wish he'd put it back.

At that moment, a big group of people walk in through the door. There are at least ten of them, and they're loud and drunk. Both Dean and I turn towards them and then exchange a glance. They take up so much space, and the peaceful spell that was over us starts to break.

"You want to get out of here?" Dean says as he turns his head back to me. I feel my lips curl into a smile and I nod.

"Definitely."

We walk back up the stairs into the fresh night air. Dean's Bentley is gleaming under the street lights. Instead of heading towards it, he motions down the street.

"There's a nice park down here. You want to go for a walk?"

"Sure," I say. We turn towards the park and our hands slip into each other. My heart jumps in my chest as our fingers intertwine and the heat of his body gets a bit closer. Everything feels so natural with him. I clear my throat.

"How's your arm feeling?"

"It's fine. Just a scratch," he says with a grin. "Well, broken in two places but you know. I'm tough."

"Rub some dirt in it," I say with a grin.

"Exactly," he laughs. "Can't even feel it."

We walk in silence for a few moments. It's a peaceful silence. We're both wrapped in our own thoughts but our hands are still together and our steps are synchronized. The peacefulness in my heart from before is still there, but there's something else inside me too. A warmth, or a spark, or something traveling up my arm and straight to my core. I clear my throat.

"So why did your dinner get cut short? Did anything happen?"

I feel Dean's body stiffen beside me and he takes a slow, deep breath. He lets out all the air before speaking.

"They'd invited someone I didn't want to see," he finally responds. I nod, sensing that he doesn't want to be asked any more questions. I think about what he said earlier, that he'd been through something similar to me. Was it his ex-fiancée?

Why would she be at his parent's house? A tendril of jealousy starts curdling in my stomach as I think of another woman getting close to Dean. I shake my head, trying to talk some sense into myself.

I only met him today. We don't know each other, and he definitely doesn't owe me anything. He obviously has a history with this woman, and plus, I don't even know if it was her that was there! I'm jumping to conclusions. I just met the guy and I just sent off my divorce papers. I need to relax.

As if he can sense the turbulent thoughts in my head, he squeezes my hand gently. We turn down a pathway into the park and Dean speaks in a low voice.

"I'm glad that the dinner got cut short," he says, "because it meant I could come and see you."

My heart starts jumping in my chest as we slow to a stop and Dean turns to face me. His sling is pinning his arm between us, and he runs his other hand across my cheek and along my jaw. I tilt my chin up towards him and part my lips as my heart bounces in my chest. The spark between my legs ignites as he dips his lips towards mine.

His kiss set my whole body on fire. The instant his lips crush against mine and his fingers tangle into my hair, I feel myself melting into him. I peel myself away from his broken arm and wrap my arms around his neck. He pulls me in closer and kisses me like I've never been kissed before. Our lips dance together and our bodies fuse together as we stand under the streetlights in the cool night air. He's the only man beside Ronnie I've kissed in years, but I can tell that this kiss is different. It's more intense and more passionate than any other. His hand grips the back of my head and I sink my fingers into his shoulders, his neck, his back. I run my hands through the hair at the nape of his neck and taste the sweetness of the champagne on his lips.

Finally, we pull apart and Dean nods to his cast.

"Stupid thing," he growls with a chuckle. "If there was ever a moment that I wanted full use of both my hands it would be right now."

I smile and trail my fingers down his arm and over his cast. "We wouldn't be here if it weren't for this thing," I say. Dean grunts in agreement and dips his head towards me for another kiss.

15

DEAN

SINCE I'VE BROKEN up with Victoria, I've kissed plenty of women. I go out at night with Jacob or one of the boys, we find women and hook up with them. They wrap their arms around me and we kiss all night, or at least until I got them undressed.

But now, with Sam, it's different. It's like our bodies are melting together, like we're closer than I've ever been to a woman even though we're fully clothed and out in public. I don't feel the chill of the air, I don't hear anyone walk past us, I don't hear the faint sounds of the traffic. All that exists is her and me and our lips. I wrap my fingers into her hair and pull her closer. She lets out a soft moan and my body starts blazing.

Sam pulls her head back and stares into my eyes.

"Whoa," she breathes.

I chuckle softly. "I know."

"I haven't kissed anyone like that..." her eyes glaze over as she thinks. "In I don't know how long."

"It's good," I growl before dipping my head back down

towards hers. She moans again and my cock throbs between my legs. I want her so bad. I don't know if I've ever wanted a woman as much as I do now. I pulls her even closer. She wraps her arms around my neck and her chest hits my arm.

The pain shoots up to my shoulder and I wince, pulling away.

"Aah," I say. "This fucking thing."

"Sorry!" Sam says. "I forgot."

"So did I," I grin. She smiles and takes a step back. "I got carried away."

"We're not doing much walking," she says as she glances at me sideways.

"Kissing it better."

She laughs and nods towards the path. We keep walking as she interlaces her fingers in mine. Our arms swing gently between us, and I feel a constant current of energy connecting us. My cock feels hard and heavy between my legs. It rubs against my thighs with every step, like a constant reminder of my burning desire.

"I could get used to this city," Sam says. "It's not as hectic as I thought it would be. I thought I'd be overwhelmed but I'm kind of enjoying it. I like walking around and having no one know who I am."

"Anonymity can be good," I reply. "It can get lonely sometimes though. Sometimes I feel like I'm surrounded by millions of people but there's not a single one of them that I know."

Sam chuckles softly and shakes her head. "I guess it's the same everywhere. When I left Lexington I felt like I was being suffocated. I understood why Jess left when she was young. All the stares and the whispers about me. You'd have thought I was the one who cheated."

Her voice is bitter and I glance over to see her face drawn. Her lips, usually so plump, are pulled into a thin line across her face. My heart pulls in my chest and I want to help her somehow, but I don't know what to say. I just nod and grunt. Sam shakes her head.

"Sorry," she says. "Isn't the first rule of dating 'don't talk about your ex'? Clearly I'm out of practice," she laughs.

"I don't mind. I like listening to you talk," I say. The words surprise me. The fact that I'm walking hand-in-hand with a woman surprises me. The fact that I'm enjoying it as much as I am surprises me.

My thoughts drift to Victoria and all the bitter months that led up to the end. I don't remember the last time I actually enjoyed a woman's company. Is this what it's supposed to feel like?

"I think you're really brave," I say. Sam glances at me and scoffs.

"Right," she says.

"I mean it! You're going through the toughest thing anyone should go through. It's no fault of your own, and here you are in a brand new city making something new of yourself. A lot of people would just wallow in self-pity and crumble after something like that. I know people who have been through divorces that haven't been the same since."

Sam sighs. "I've done a lot of wallowing," she admits. She shakes her head and laughs. "A *lot* of wallowing. It hasn't been pretty."

"I doubt that," I say. "I can't imagine you not being pretty."

Sam glances at me and lets out a laugh. She nudges me with her elbow. "Very smooth."

"I try," I say with a grin. I look down and meet her eye for an instant and my heart grows in my chest. She turns her head and takes a deep breath.

"It's such a beautiful night."

"It is," I reply. My heart starts beating as I think of what I'm about to ask. Our loop through the park is almost done and I can see the street where I parked. All I want to do is bring her back to my place. I clear my throat. "My apartment building has a nice balcony. We could grab some wine and go up there? There's a beautiful view of the city."

Sam looks at me, tilting her head to the side. She smiles sadly and shakes her head. "I shouldn't."

"Why not?" I say, maybe a bit too quickly. Sam squeezes my hand slightly and she stares straight ahead as we turn back onto the road.

"I've had a wonderful evening, Dean, I really have. A wonderful day, actually," she says. She pauses and takes a deep breath and then shakes her head. "I'd love to go back to your place but I'm just not ready. It's too soon."

My voice is soft when I reply, squeezing her hand back. "We don't have to have sex, Sam. I just want to spend more time with you."

She finally looks at me again and tilts her head. It looks like she's studying my face as her eyes squint the tiniest bit. Finally she smiles softly.

"I wouldn't trust myself," she admits, laughing. "I don't want to do anything I'll regret."

"You're probably right," I say, swinging my arm across her shoulders. Her arm crosses over across my back to hang on to my waist. "Let's just take it slow."

She doesn't say anything, but she leans her head against my shoulder. We walk up to the car and I find my keys in my pocket to unlock it. When I pull the passenger's side door open, she puts her hand on top of it and looks at me.

"Thank you, Dean. Thank you for understanding."

"Don't be silly, Sam." I pause, and take a step towards her. I run my finger along her cheek and tuck a strand of that rich brown hair behind her ear. "I like you. I'm not going to pressure you to do anything."

She smiles and I dip my lips down to hers. This time we kiss softly, maybe more softly than I've ever kissed anyone. Our mouths brush against each other and she parts her lips to let me kiss her ever so slightly deeper. I groan and pull away.

"This isn't making it any easier to say goodnight to you," I say.

Sam laughs. "Oops," she says with a wink before turning to the open door and sliding into the seat. I close the door behind her and let out a sigh. I try to walk around the front of the car normally, struggling to hide the fact that my cock is rock hard between my legs.

16

SAMANTHA

Saying goodbye to Dean was difficult, but when I close Jess's front door and lean against it with my eyes closed, I'm glad I didn't go to his place.

I wanted to. Obviously, I mean, *come on*. What girl wouldn't want to be with him. I was so close to giving in and going to his place and letting myself have a wild night with him, but I couldn't. I just sent my divorce papers to the lawyer today, it feels wrong to go to bed with someone else.

All I need is some time to think. I don't know if he's a rebound, or a distraction, or a way of me getting over Ronnie. Or maybe, and this scares me almost more than anything else, maybe he's the real thing. Maybe he is as caring and kind as he seems to be.

Jess surprises me when her head pops up around the corner.

"Tell. Me. Everything," she says in a hushed whisper.

"I didn't think you'd still be up."

"I couldn't sleep," she admits. "Come on, you want some tea? Wine?"

"Tea sounds good," I say, following her to the kitchen. I sit down and she starts boiling the water and then turns to me.

"So...???" She looks at me expectantly. I laugh and then shrug.

"It was fun. It was great! We went to a jazz bar and then went out for a walk."

"I saw that car he picked you up in. A Bentley? Was that a rental? Who is this guy?"

I laugh. "I'm not sure," I say as I shake my head. "He said his father is an investment banker, and I'll be honest I'm not exactly sure what that means."

"Neither am I," Jess says as she drops a cup of tea in front of me. "So?? I thought for sure I wouldn't see you until tomorrow. Will you see him again?"

"Yeah," I reply. "Well, I hope so. We kissed."

Jess makes a noise and gives me an approving nod. "Good girl," she says. "As you should."

I laugh. "It was nice. I mean, it was better than nice. He did that thing where he wraps his hand around my head and like pulled me closer. Do you know what I mean?"

"Mmm," Jess says approvingly, nodding as she takes a sip. "That's hot."

"So hot," I reply with a laugh. "I couldn't think straight."

"And you didn't want to sleep with him?"

"I mean, yeah, obviously I did. I do!" I laugh. "He invited me back to his place."

"You said no?!"

"I'm not ready, Jess. I just sent the papers to the lawyer today. I'm not even officially divorced yet."

Jess shrugs. "That doesn't mean anything."

"I know, but I just don't feel ready. I don't know how to explain it. It's like I'm still mourning the end of my marriage.

It feels wrong to just jump into bed with someone else." I hold up my hand. "I know what you're going to say. You're going to say it didn't feel wrong for Ronnie, but I'm not like him. I don't know, I can't put it into words."

Jess smiles. "I wasn't going to say that. I get it. Don't get me wrong, I definitely want you to bang him, but if you're not ready yet then that's okay. I don't think you have to wait for the official divorce to go through though, if that's what you're waiting for."

"It's not," I say as I take a sip. "I don't know what I'm waiting for. Even when I was kissing him, like I was loving it and it was so hot and I was more turned on than I've been in years. But it still felt like I shouldn't be doing it. Or like, I was going to get caught. Does that make sense?"

"Yeah," Jess says. She takes a deep breath. "I'm sorry you're going through this, Sam. I thought your wedding was the real deal."

"So did I," I say, but the words catch in my throat. I shake my head and blink my eyes a few times. "I don't want to cry. I just met an amazing, sexy, respectful man that wants to see me again. I should be happy!"

"Did he seem upset when you turned him down?"

"No! Not at all. He was so nice about it, it seemed like he really understood why I said no. I mean, when we were kissing I think I felt a boner," I say with a grin. Jess bursts out laughing and claps her hands before bringing her hands to her mouth.

"The twins are asleep," she explains and then grins at me. "You could feel it?! How did it feel?" she asks. "Like..?" she pulls her two index fingers apart. "Tell me when to stop," she says and wiggles her eyebrows at me. I laugh.

"I don't know, it's not like I felt it up. I mean, I could feel it through his pants so it's not like it was small."

Jess grins. "I can't wait for you to get laid."

"Me too," I laugh. "Who knows, it might happen sooner than later."

"I hope so," she says. "So when are you seeing him again?"

"I'm not sure, we haven't made any plans. Hey, Jess," I start, looking at her hesitantly. I take a deep breath and try to ignore the nervousness in my chest. She nods her head expectantly.

"What is it?"

"I was thinking I might stay in New York a bit longer than I thought. Would it... would it be alright if I stayed here?" I ask, finding the courage to pull my eyes up to hers. "Only until I find my own place! I promise. I'll pay you rent."

Jess laughs and stands up to move towards me. She wraps me in a hug. "Of course, Sam. Stay as long as you want. I told you that! We have an extra bedroom for a reason, and you're great with the twins."

She sits back down and grins at me. "He's had quite the effect on you," she teases. I feel my cheeks blush immediately and I shake my head.

"It's okay," Jess says with a laugh. "I'm happy for you. You deserve to be happy." She smiles at me and I feel my heart grow in my chest. "You also deserve to get laid," she says. "Like, properly laid."

I laugh. "I can arrange that."

"Good. Alright, I'll see you in the morning. Just leave those mugs in the sink, I'll get them in the morning."

"See you tomorrow."

Jess gives me another hug and goes back to her bedroom.

I sigh and look around the kitchen. I can hear the noise of cars outside and a distant siren. I shake my head. I guess I'll be trying the city life for a while.

17

DEAN

I RESIST the urge to text her as soon as I get home. I glance out the floor to ceiling windows and imagine Sam's face if she were to see the skyline from up here. I'm sure she would be blown away, it's a spectacular view. I pull out my phone and walk out to the balcony, taking a panoramic picture of the skyline. I find Sam's number in my phone and send her the snap.

A few minutes later, I get a photo message back from her. I open it up and see her face, surrounded by pillows and blankets. She has a soft smile on her face and I immediately wish I was there beside her. My cock throbs again and I sigh. Even seeing her face or thinking of the way she moves sets my body on fire.

I write a quick text to respond.

Dean: Have a good sleep. Dinner tomorrow?

I press send and walk back inside, closing the sliding glass door behind me. I slump down on the sofa and try to ignore the butterflies crashing around my stomach. Why would I be nervous about asking her out? We've already been out together!

My phone buzzes and I practically pounce on it.

Sam: Sounds good xx goodnight

I send her a quick goodnight and lean back in my couch. I let out all the air from my lungs and shake my head. Where did she come from? Why is my head spinning so much? Why is my cock throbbing constantly?

Well, I mean, I know the answer to that one. My hand drifts to my crotch and I trace the outline of my cock with my fingers over my jeans. I run my hands up and down the length of my shaft and groan as it starts to get harder.

I pull out my phone and look at her picture. Her eyes are half-closed, and I try to see what she's wearing. I can't see anything except her face and shoulder, and I close my eyes to imagine her naked body. My head fills with images of Sam. I think of the way her shirt hugged her curves. I could just see the outline of her bra peeking above the lace when she leaned over. I think of the way my fingers sank into her waist, or the way her face brightened whenever she laughed. I think of her kiss, and how her body felt when it was pressed against mine. I could feel every curve as she wrapped her fingers around my neck and pulled herself closer to me.

I start thinking about things that haven't happened, and I unzip my pants to finally free my cock. I imagine what she would look like if she were here in front of me. Maybe she'd kneel down and take my cock between those perfect lips. I could touch her breasts and wrap my fingers into her hair as I watched her take inch after inch of my cock in her mouth.

A groan escapes my lips as I wrap my fingers around my shaft. Pretty soon I'm imagining Sam all over me. I'm picturing what it would feel like to plunge my cock deep inside her and wondering what she tastes like when she's sopping wet. My hand moves up and down and I groan as I close my eyes, waiting for that sweet release.

It's the thought of her bouncing on my cock that makes me come. I imagine myself exactly in this position on the sofa, and Sam bouncing up and down as she rides me. I imagine running my hands all over her body and feeling her walls contract around my shaft. I imagine her wetness running down between my legs as she plunges my cock deep inside her.

My balls tighten up towards my shaft and I push my shirt up my chest. I come hard, letting my seed shoot out of my cock onto my stomach and chest. I groan as I feel the release of my orgasm and my whole body tenses and then relaxes. I take a few deep breaths and sigh. My body is twitching until finally that familiar post-orgasmic calm washes over me.

As good as that felt, I know it would be nothing compared to the real thing. It was more just relieving the pressure in my balls than getting any real pleasure from it. I sit up and look around for a cloth or a tissue. Of course, there's nothing, and I need to jog to the bathroom to clean up. Once I'm done, I splash some water on my face and take a deep breath.

I understand why she didn't want to come back to my place, and I respect it, but damn, I wish she was here. My cock isn't permanently semi-hard anymore, like it's been all evening, but the rest of me feels empty too. I wander back to the kitchen as my stomach growls. I haven't eaten in hours. I open the fridge and look inside, sighing as I pull out some ham for a sandwich.

When I first left my ex, I was heartbroken but also glad

for the space. I loved being my own man and being able to do whatever I wanted. I loved having the whole apartment to myself, I loved coming and going and bringing home whoever I wanted.

Now, all of a sudden this apartment seems cold and empty. I slap some mustard on the bread and put the ham on top of it. I look back in the fridge for cheese and let out another sigh. I'm not sure what to do with myself now, it feels almost lonely in here. I put the other piece of bread on top of my sandwich and stare at it for a couple seconds. If I'm being completely honest with myself, I don't want to be eating a ham sandwich by myself on a Saturday night. I want to be out with a beautiful woman, having a delicious meal, and then coming back here and fucking her brains out.

I take my first bite and groan in satisfaction. I shouldn't blame the sandwich. The sandwich is delicious. If Sam were here having a post-orgasm ham sandwich with me it would be the best meal of my life. I know what these feelings are, and they've been building up inside me ever since my breakup.

It's loneliness, plain and simple. The single life is great, but it's lonely. A ham sandwich by yourself doesn't taste as good as a ham sandwich with a beautiful, intelligent, witty woman. I pull out my phone and take a picture of the half-eaten sandwich, unable to resist sending it to Sam.

Dean: *Wild Saturday night over here.*

I know I shouldn't bombard her with texts. I should be playing it cool, and letting her sleep, but I can't. I want to see her again tomorrow, and the next day, and the next. I want to know what she's thinking and I want to make her laugh. I want to share everything with her, even this stupid sandwich.

I'm surprised when my phone buzzes. I open it up to see a

photo message from Sam. I open it quickly and burst out laughing when I see a picture of a bowl of cereal.

Sam: Cereal party at my place. Bring Cheerios.

I know she's joking but I'd be at her door with a box of Cheerios in an instant, all she'd have to do is tell me to come over.

18

SAMANTHA

"Two nights in a row!" Jess exclaims with a smile. "I'd swear you're trying to get away from me."

"Just zip me up," I answer with a laugh. I'm holding the clasp of my dress closed at the back of my neck as Jess zips up the back. It's the nicest thing I brought with me, a simple black cocktail dress. My heart is thumping in my chest and I smooth my hands down the front of the dress. I turn around and Jess nods in approval.

"You look hot," she says. She sighs and shakes her head. "I wish I was being whisked around to all the nicest spots in New York."

I laugh. "You had your time," I say. "It's not like Owen hasn't spoiled you."

"I know, I know. It's just hard with twins."

"I'll babysit one night," I say as I slip some earrings into my ears. "Just let me know. You guys deserve a night off."

Jess smiles at me. "Thanks Sam, that sounds great, actually. What time is Clifford—I mean, Dean picking you up?"

"Should be any minute now, I think."

"Is he bringing that car again? Would it be weird if I asked him to take me for a drive around the block in it?"

"Yes, that would be weird," I reply with a laugh. Jess just shrugs and grins at me. The doorbell rings and we look at each other. Jess's eyebrows shoot up to her hairline and my heart starts doing backflips in my chest. Suddenly, thousands of butterflies are crashing around my stomach and I feel like I've forgotten how to speak English.

"You look great," Jess says. "Come on."

Owen has already opened the door when we walk towards the front of the house. He's shaking hands with Dean. My jaw almost drops when I see him. He's wearing a simple black suit with a white shirt. He's still wearing his sling, and the end of his cast is sticking out of his shirt sleeve. The top button is undone and I can see a glimpse of his muscular chest. A shiver runs down my spine as my thoughts flick back to the hospital parking lot. His hair is perfectly tousled and his beard is trimmed. He looks incredible, and the heat between my legs instantly flares.

"So sorry again about yesterday," I hear Owen say. "I don't know what got into Matt, he's never hit anyone like that before."

"Don't mention it," Dean says with a laugh. "It'll just be another story to tell. It's not as bad as the time one kid threw her dirty diaper at me."

Owen chuckles and gestures to invite him in. Dean takes a step in and lifts his eyes up to me. His eyes brighten the tiniest bit and his lips part ever so slightly. I take the last few steps towards him and reach up to kiss his cheek.

"Hey," I say simply.

"Hey," he responds. "You look beautiful." His eyes are shining as he looks me up and down one more time. The most delicious tingle travels with his eyes as he takes in every inch of my body. My cheeks start to blush and I turn to Jess and Owen.

"See you guys later," I say a little too loudly. Jess nods and smiles before giving me a hug with one arm. Dean and I walk out the door. As soon as the door closes I turn to Dean. "Is it just me or did it feel like we were teenagers going to prom? Jess and Owen were standing there like proud parents."

Dean laughs and a shiver travels up my spine again. "Yeah, I got that sense as well. I didn't mind though, it brought me back to my youth. Makes me feel like I'm being naughty or something."

I laugh as he takes my hand and helps me down the steps. He opens the passenger's side door for me and I slide into his gleaming black Bentley once again. I watch him walk over to the driver's side and get in. He turns to me and smiles before leaning over and reaching his hand to my cheek. He kisses me gently, pressing his lips to mine and groaning.

"Had to do that," he says with a grin.

"I'm not complaining," I reply as I try to control the beating of my heart. He smiles a bit wider and turns on the car.

"Where are you taking me?" I ask.

Dean smiles as he pulls out onto the street. "It's a surprise. You'll love it."

My heart hasn't slowed down a bit as we drive a bit further. I slide my hand onto his thigh and he tenses it slightly and then relaxes. For just a second he takes his hand off the steering wheel and brushes the tips of my fingers with his. He goes back to driving and I wonder if he'd hold my hand if both his arms were functional. We drive a bit further until we get to a huge well-lit building.

Dean pulls up in front of the portico and a valet in a fancy uniform opens the door for me. I step out and he nods before closing the door and going around to the other side. I watch as Dean hands him the keys smoothly and then comes to join me. I try to keep the awe off my face when I see how normal this is for him. He hooks my arm into his and walks me towards the door.

Before we can touch the front doors, they swing open and another man nods to me. I smile at him and glide through the doors. We're guided towards the elevators and let up to the top floor. Dean squeezes my arm in his and looks over at me. He winks.

"What do you think so far?" he asks.

"It's a far cry from Lexington, Virginia," I say with a laugh. "I'm used to opening my own doors."

"Not tonight," he says with a smile.

The elevator doors open to a magnificent restaurant. Every table is beautifully set with rich tablecloths and gleaming silverware. There are candles flickering on each table. On every single wall there are floor-to-ceiling windows showing off New York's sparkling skyline. We're led by yet another smartly-dressed employee to our table. It's beside the window and I gasp as we get closer. I can see everything from up here—all the lights and cars and movement below us. The table itself has a vase with a single long-stem rose in it, and a few rose petals strewn across the table. The waiter appears immediately with sparkling water and a list of wines.

Dean hands it to me and I glance at the long wine menu. It hardly even looks like English to me. I look up at him and shrug as I laugh.

"You choose," I say.

Dean nods and glances at the menu for no longer than a

couple seconds before asking for one of the wines. The waiter disappears and I shake my head.

"I love how you thought I'd be able to choose the wine," I say with a laugh. "Have you forgotten where I'm from?"

Dean laughs. "Maybe I have," he replies. "You seem at home over here."

"You make me feel comfortable," I reply.

Dean smiles and adjusts his sling, sighing.

"I wish this thing was more comfortable," he says. "Would you mind helping me take this jacket off?"

"Not this again," I say with a laugh. "It worked once, it's not going to work again. We're in public, Dean, get a grip!"

Dean laughs and shakes his head. "I promise to stay fully clothed."

I make an exaggerated sigh and laugh as I get up. I help him unclasp the sling and slide his jacket off, hanging it up behind his chair. He puts the sling back on and I tie it off, helping him sit down again. I make my way back to my chair and sit down across from him.

"There. And that's as much undressing of you that I'll be doing tonight," I say in a serious tone as I hold up my finger in front of me.

Dean flicks his eyes at me and the corner of his mouth curls upwards. "That's disappointing," he growls. Before I can reply, the waiter reappears with a bottle of wine. He presents it to Dean with a flourish and I watch as he tastes the wine and nods. The waiter turns to me and fills my glass and then Dean's. My heart is still thumping and the heat between my legs is growing hotter by the second. Earlier I swore I'd take things slow, but that resolve is weakening with every minute that goes by.

19

DEAN

I try to keep my hand steady as I lift my glass up to touch it to Sam's. Every time she looks at me I feel a current of energy passing through my body. She is so beautiful I can hardly look at her. When she slid my jacket off, I could feel her fingers running over my arms. All I wanted to do was press her body against mine and take her straight back to my apartment.

She tilts her head to the side and frowns as she smiles at me. "What?" she asks.

I frown. "What?" I reply.

She laughs. "Why are you looking at me like that?"

"Like what?"

"I don't know... like that."

I laugh and shrug. "You look beautiful, is all."

"Well don't get used to it," she says with a grin. "I'm a country girl at heart and this glitz and glamour won't stick."

I grin. "I'm not trying to change you."

"Good." She tilts her head to the side and looks at me curiously. "What are you trying to do?"

Her question surprises me. She's staring at me with those glittering green eyes and I can't help but hesitate before I speak. I take a sip of my wine and put the glass back down gently before lifting my eyes back up to hers. She's still staring at me, with a hint of a grin playing on her lips.

"I'm trying to get to know you," I finally say. It seems like a weak answer. I don't know what I'm trying to do. I'm trying to spend more time with her. I'm trying to get into bed with her, but not really. Not only that. I want to be closer to her. I can't put it into words, I just feel myself drawn to her. She nods slowly and smiles.

"Do you usually go after recently divorced women? I must be a bit younger than your usual prey."

I laugh. "Prey? Do you think that's all you are to me?"

"I don't know what I am to you. I only met you yesterday but somehow we've been on two dates already."

"That's true. Well, to be honest, no I don't go after recently divorced women. I don't go after many women at all." She scoffs and rolls her eyes and I think of all the one night stands I've had since I left Victoria. "I don't go on dates with many women," I correct myself.

"Right." She's still looking at me and I feel the urge to be honest with her. My eyes trail over her face, from her eyes to the smattering of freckles across her nose, down to those luscious lips. My gaze lingers over her lips until I finally look at her eyes again. She's nothing like the cookie-cutter women in this city. She's so *real* and I want to be real with her too.

I take a deep breath. "I was supposed to get married next month. The date was set, the venue was booked. My mother had invited the whole city. And then...". My voice trails off.

"And then?" she asks softly.

"And then I walked in on my fiancee with another man in

my bed." Sam's eyebrows draw together and her mouth drops open. "And then that was it," I finish.

"Dean, I'm so sorry."

"It's fine. It's over now, even if my parents don't believe it."

"Did they like her?"

They'd been planning the union since I was born. Their business plans were riding on our marriage, and they blame me for ruining it.

"Yeah," I say. "They did."

Sam nods slowly. "I'm sorry."

"You don't have to apologize, it wasn't your fault. You've been through the same. Worse, even, you were already married!"

"I didn't walk in on him," she says. She takes a deep breath and lifts her eyes up to mine. "This is the first time I've been able to talk about it without feeling like I'm going to burst into tears. It's nice to meet someone who gets it."

"I get it," I say bitterly, swirling the red wine in my glass and watching it drip down the sides. "For the first month I had that dirty feeling in my stomach like I was constantly on the verge of throwing up. Then I drank every day for a month after that. I swore I'd never trust a woman again."

"Do you still feel that way?" Sam's voice is so low I hardly hear her question. That doesn't change the weight of it. I can hear the question behind it, where she's asking *would you ever trust me*. I lift my eyes up to hers and try to smile.

"I'm starting to think differently now," I say.

The waiter appears with our food and Sam makes an appreciative moan. I flick my eyes up to her as my cock twitches at the noise, but her eyes are glued on her plate. The filet mignon steak is steaming in front of her and she grins as she finally looks at me.

"This looks amazing," she breathes.

"I know," I say, looking at the way her dress dips down just enough to reveal the curve of her breast. She glances up at me and smiles.

"Bon appetit!"

We tuck in to our food and for a few minutes there's nothing but groans of appreciation. Finally Sam looks up at me and shakes her head.

"You've outdone yourself, Dean, this is unreal."

I laugh. "All I did was bring you here. The staff did all the work."

"Still. This is the best meal I've had in years." She pokes a bite of steak with her fork and chews, closing her eyes as she tastes the meat. My cock twitches again as I watch her, and I shift in my seat to adjust myself. I chuckle.

"Wait until dessert. They make the best fudge brownie I've ever had."

Sam's eyes flick open and she stares at me. "Brownies are my favorite dessert of. All. Time."

"Me too," I grin. "There's another thing we have in common."

"A slightly more pleasant one," she laughs as she takes another bite of her meal. I watch the fork travel to her mouth and can't look away as her lips surround the meat. My thoughts flick back to last night, alone on my sofa with nothing but my thoughts. This is way too close to what I was imagining, and my cock is rock hard under the table. I clear my throat and stare at my plate, trying to distract myself from the appreciative noises that Sam is making. I don't even think she realizes how much she's turning me on.

Somehow, I make it through the rest of the meal and past dessert without exploding in my pants. We stand up to leave and I let my hand drift to the small of her back. She still smells floral and sweet as we walk out of the restaurant. Once we're in the elevator, she turns to me and crawls her fingers up my chest. Her head tilts up towards mine and I press my hand on her back to pull her into me.

Our lips meet and she melts her whole body into mine. Her hands grip the collar of my shirt as she pulls me closer, dipping her tongue into my mouth as my whole body is set on fire by her kiss. We pull apart as the elevator dings and the door opens. My car is waiting for us outside the door. Sam smiles at me and slips her hand into mine as we walk towards it.

"Thank you for a wonderful evening, Dean."

"I can't tempt you with a nightcap, can I?"

She smiles again, more sadly this time. She shakes her head slowly and her hair flows on either side of her face. "Not tonight."

My heart sinks ever so slightly but I nod and smile. The valet opens her door. The second her hand leaves mine to get in the car I feel like something is missing from me. I make my way to my side of the car and get in, trying not to let my disappointment show. The evening is already over and soon I'll be alone again.

20

SAMANTHA

I CAN STILL TASTE Dean's kiss on my lips when I crawl into bed. I lay back on the pillows and stare up at the ceiling. I sigh, wondering if I should be holding back this much. All I want to do is go back to his place and spend the night with him.

It feels so good to be with Dean. He makes me laugh, he makes me feel safe, and I feel like he understands me. He's been through what I've been through. He knows what it feels like to be betrayed.

Still, it's so soon. I don't want to jump into anything and regret it. I haven't slept with anyone but Ronnie in so long, the thought of getting naked in front of Dean is simultaneously exciting and terrifying.

I'm not ready.

I'm still a married woman, after all. Until I get the word from my lawyer that everything has gone through, it feels wrong to be going out with Dean.

Well, not wrong, exactly. Everything about being with Dean feels *right*. It's just strange to change my whole way of thinking.

I was ready to be a wife forever. I was ready to be Ronnie's for the rest of my days, and now it's all over. It's hard to get used to.

Maybe Jess is right. I should just enjoy this for what it is. A bit of flirtation, some attention, some making out. If I don't want to have sex with Dean, then I won't. If I do, I will.

Simple.

Sort of. I close my eyes and blow the air out of my nose as Dean's body appears on my eyelids. I think of him undressing in the hospital parking lot, and how broad and muscular his chest was. I think of the way his eyes gleamed after he kissed me goodbye tonight, and the way his hand felt on the small of my back. He'd inched his fingers towards the cleft of my ass cheeks and my whole body was pulsing with desire.

I wonder what it would feel like to have his skin on my skin, to have his fingers trailing along my spine and have his hands gripping my ass.

Well, his hand. For the next few weeks he only has one working arm.

I squeeze my eyes shut and try to steady my breath. My heartbeat is speeding up just thinking about him, and I need to get to sleep. Tomorrow I start my job search, and I see if I'll be able to stay in this city for longer than a few weeks.

I WAKE up to the sounds of tiny feet running down the hallway. I open my eyes to see the door to my bedroom open and a tiny head poking through. It's Michelle, with her usual mischievous grin. I smile and sit up on my elbows.

"Morning, beautiful."

She gurgles and walks towards me with her arms outstretched. I grab her and hoist her onto the bed as she giggles and pokes my chest with her two-year-old fingers. I laugh.

"Michelle!" I hear Jess's voice come down the hall. She appears in the door. "Oh, gosh, sorry Sam. I thought she was right behind me. I didn't mean to wake you."

"It's alright, I was just getting up," I say as Michelle slides down and runs towards her mother. Jess takes her hand and leads her towards the door.

"There's coffee in the kitchen," she calls out behind her shoulder. "How was your date?"

"It was great," I say. Jess smiles and ushers Michelle out. As usual, she's busy with the kids this morning, and I rub my eyes as I swing my legs over the edge of the bed. I'm still getting used to being in a full house like this. I wrap my housecoat around myself and head towards the kitchen.

"Morning," Owen says as he slips by me towards the door. "Jess! I'm heading out! I'll see you this evening!"

Jess appears and gives Owen a quick kiss. I grab the pot of coffee and pour myself a mug. There's a toddler between my legs and I laugh as I shift over and make my way to the table. It's almost like I'm a piece of furniture, or like they've all accepted me as part of the family already.

I pull out my phone and scroll through my various social media accounts as I drink my coffee. Jess comes back in the kitchen and tries to wrangle the twins into their high chairs. She moves swiftly and efficiently and pretty soon the twins are seated with some food in front of them. Jess sighs and grabs herself a coffee as I glance back at my phone.

A text comes through as I look at it. Ronnie's name pops up and my chest feels hollow.

Ronnie: Didn't take you long to sign those papers. Bitch.

I can feel the blood draining from my face as I read the words over and over. Jess clears her throat.

"What's wrong, Sam?"

I glance from my phone up to her and shake my head. "Ronnie texted me."

"What did he say? Actually, you know what, I don't want to know. Is it bad? Screenshot it, then delete it and ignore. Seriously, Sam. Don't engage."

My throat tightens and I nod. "He called me a bitch."

"Asshole," she spits, and then glances at her twins. They're engrossed in their food and she purses her lips. "Don't worry about him, Sam. You're done with him."

"I know. It's just hard. It's still raw."

"I get it." She takes a sip of coffee then sits up straighter. "You job hunting today? That's exciting!"

"Yeah, I emailed my boss from the organization last week. She gave me some contact details for an after school non-profit here in the city, so I'll give them a call. She said she'd put in a good word for me."

"That's great, Sam! See? You don't need Lexington or Ronnie or anyone else. Here you are, and within three days you've got a guy chasing after you and good prospects for a job. Don't worry about that asshole trying to bring you down to his level."

I nod. "Yeah. You're right." I force a smile and nod again. "Yeah."

"Okay, I'm bringing the kids to daycare. You'll be alright today? I've got a full schedule."

"I'll be fine, Jess, don't worry about me."

Within a few minutes, she's back up and getting the kids ready to leave. I shake my head and then get up and try to help her. I end up just getting in the way, and before I know it she's out the door an the house is quiet again. I take a deep breath to enjoy the sudden stillness.

I pull out my phone and find the phone number my boss gave me. With a deep breath, I press the 'call' button and hope for the best.

21

DEAN

When I walk into the office it somehow feels different than it did last week. I'm wearing the same suit, and everyone is sitting at the same desks, but something has changed. I say good morning to the receptionist and make my way to my desk. It's all how I left it on Friday, but it feels fresher or newer than it did before. It's like the whole world is a little bit brighter, or all the colors are a bit more vibrant, or the air tastes that little bit sweeter.

I sit down at my desk and stretch my neck from side to side as my laptop boots up. I hum gently to myself and let a smile play over my lips. I haven't felt this good in months, even with a broken arm.

The feeling dulls a bit when I hear my father's voice across the room.

"Dean! My office. Now."

A few heads turn towards me as I look over at him. He doesn't even make eye contact with me, he just keeps walking towards the big office in the back corner of the room. I glance down at my screen and take a deep breath. He never asks anything, only commands. I get up slowly and smooth my shirt down and readjust my sling before following him towards the office.

"Close the door," he barks as I walk in. I do as he says and turn back to him. He motions to a chair across from his desk and then rests his elbows on the arms of his chair and tents his fingers across his chest. I sit down and try to act casual as I wait for him to speak. When he doesn't, I clear my throat.

"Anything I can do for you?"

My father's eyes darken as he stares at me across the desk. "You upset your mother on Saturday," he says slowly. "And that means you upset me."

"Dad—" I start and he holds up a hand. He's wearing his wedding band and an expensive watch that glints as he moves. He slowly lowers his hand back down and stares at me again.

"Victoria did you a favor, coming back to the house like that."

"She fucked another guy *in our bed*," I spit. "What the fuck do you want me to do? Pretend it never happened?"

"Grow up, Dean," my father says with a sigh. "Do you think marriage is about love? Do you think this is a fucking fairy tale? For people like you and I, marriage is big business. And your marriage in particular," he says with gravity. "Is *very* important."

I swallow and shift in my seat. I can still see Victoria's face when I walked in on her. I look down at my father's desk and shake my head.

"I can't do it."

"Dean, this has been in the works for over twenty years. The Erkharts have been very successful politically. This is our chance to move the family to real power. Do you understand that? We have the money and they have the connections. You could be something."

"What if I don't want to 'be something', Dad, did you ever think of that?"

"Are you going to be a clown for the rest of your life? I mean that literally and figuratively."

I bristle and my father sighs.

"Dean, son, I get that you wanted to volunteer some time, I really do. But this is your future we're talking about. This is our whole family's future. Do you understand that you could run for office? You could be a congressman or even a governor. You could make real decisions!"

"Make decisions! You mean *you* could make decisions. You won't even let me marry who I want! You want me to marry a woman who fucking cheated on me. Do you understand that??"

My dad shakes his head slowly and sighs. "There are arrangements that you can make, Dean. Do you think your mother and I have only had each other? I married her to get my start, and I grew this firm into what it is today. Now it's your responsibility to take it to the next level."

My heart starts thumping and I can feel the heat rising in my neck. The lightness I felt this morning is gone, and in its place is the weight of the world on my shoulders. I can't believe I've been so stupid. It's not just a business deal between our two families. It's more than that. My parents want power, and Victoria is their ticket into politics. I'm supposed to go along for the ride.

I shake my head. "Find another way, dad. I'm not giving my life up for your dreams. If you want to go into politics then you fucking do it. I won't surround myself with snakes and backstabbers at work and in my own house for the sake of your power hungry dreams."

My father stiffens and his brow knits together. He stares at me with those dark eyes that I used to be so afraid of when I was a kid. He takes a deep breath.

"Think very carefully about what you're saying, Dean."

"I've thought about it. I'm going to live *my* life the way that *I* want to!"

"In that case, pack your desk up. Security will escort you out of the building."

He straightens some papers on his desk and turns to his computer. My jaw is hanging open as I try to process what he's just said. Did he just fire me?! I make a choking, gurgling sound and my father swings his dark eyes back to me.

"What's wrong, Dean? Not happy making your own decisions? I thought this is what you wanted. Have you forgotten that decisions have consequences?"

"Fine. Fuck you," I say. I know I sound like a petulant teenager but I don't care. I push myself up and stomp to my desk. I fling open the drawers and grab the few personal effects I have at work. I slide my phone into my pocket as the security guard walks up to my desk. I nod to him as he stands beside me.

"Lead the way, Rick." He grunts in response.

I can see heads turning as I'm escorted towards the elevators. There will be whispers about this for weeks to come. The boss's son got fired. They'll say all kinds of things about me, but they won't know the truth.

My father just fired me because I refused to marry the woman who cheated on me.

My head is spinning as the elevator door dings open. The

security guard walks me to the front door and I nod as I open the door.

"Thanks, Rick," I say. "It's been nice knowing you."

"Sorry about all this," he says. I shrug and walk outside. I take a deep breath and look both ways, trying to figure out what to do with myself. I pull out my phone and dial Jacob.

"Dean! What's up?"

"My dad just fired me. You want to go for a drink?"

"What? Yeah! Fuck man, are you okay?"

"I'm fine. I'll see you in 20."

22

SAMANTHA

"Wow, thank you, Beth. That's great. Tomorrow sounds good. Thanks again. Okay, bye." I hang up the phone and stare at the screen for a few minutes before jumping up and down. I dial Jess's number, and she picks up on the second ring.

"I got the job! I got the job, they want me to start tomorrow!"

"What! You didn't even interview! How is that possible? Congratulations!"

"She said she'd talked to my boss and had gotten a glowing recommendation. They need someone badly and we could treat my first two weeks as probation, like an extended interview."

"Holy shit, congrats!"

"Thanks," I say, shuffling my feet and jumping up excitedly. "Anyways, I had to tell someone. I know you're busy today, I'll let you go."

"I'll get some wine on the way home. We can have pizza or something tonight and celebrate as a family."

"Are you saying I'm part of the family now," I ask with a grin.

"You always were, Sam, you know that," she laughs. "Okay gotta go. I'll see you tonight."

I hang up the phone and take a deep breath. A smile spreads across my face. Things are starting to come together! I've never had things go so well. I've met a guy that I like, and who seems to like me back, I've found a job with almost no trouble at all, and I have a place to stay with people who care about me.

My fresh start is feeling great.

The day starts flying by. I have to go out and buy new work clothes since I didn't bring any with me and I need to make sure I've got all the paperwork for tomorrow. There's a thousand and one bits and pieces that I need to do before I start tomorrow. I'm going straight into a full-time job as an assistant program director. I have no doubt it'll be busy from the beginning.

It's not until late afternoon when I get back home that I notice the missed calls on my phone. Jess is already home and she sees me frown as I look at the screen.

"Ronnie again?" she asks with a raised eyebrow. I glance at her and shake my head.

"No, it's Dean. He's called me three times."

"He seems clingy," she says with a slight frown. "Hasn't he ever heard of playing it cool?"

I laugh. "I'm not sure. This is weird. He's calling me again!" I turn the phone around and show her the screen. Her lips stretch out into a line and she shrugs.

"You going to answer?"

"I guess so," I answer. I duck into my room and put the phone to my ear. "Dean? Is everything okay?"

"Sssam," he says. "I thought you were... I thought you were ignoring me."

"Are you drunk?" I ask, knitting my brows together. He's slurring and hard to understand. There's background noise, voices and music as if he's in a bar.

"I had a couple drinks with my friend. I got fired today."

"You got fired?! Because you were drunk??"

"No that happened—*hic*—that happened after. My own father fucking fired me."

"Oh gosh," I say, putting a hand to my forehead. "I'm sorry, Dean. You okay?"

"I'm *great*. Really great. I'm good. I want to see you."

I look up to see Jess in the doorway with her arms crossed. She has an eyebrow raised as if to ask what's going on. I nod at her and speak into the phone.

"I start a new job tomorrow, Dean, so tonight isn't so great for me. Maybe later this week?" There's a pause on the line and I frown. "Dean?"

"Okay. You're right. Sorry to bother you."

The line clicks and I look at Jess. She drops her arms by her sides and looks at me.

"What's going on?"

"He got fired this morning apparently. He's completely wasted."

"Drunk dialing you already," she says. "Not so charming after all."

I laugh and shake my head. "I just hope he's okay. He told me he worked for his father, so I don't know what would have happened for his own dad to fire him."

Jess shrugs and turns towards the kitchen. "You still want pizza tonight? I got some wine on the way home."

"Yeah," I call out after her before looking back at my phone. I find Dean's number and type a quick message.

Sam: You okay? Do you need anything?

It buzzes a few seconds later.

Dean: I fine. I think I loke yoU

I shake my head as I imagine him mashing his keyboard and trying to type when he probably can't see straight. We've all been there, just maybe not three days after meeting someone.

Sam: I like you too, Dean. Let me know if you need anything xx

I slip my phone into my pocket and head over to the kitchen. I help Jess wrangle the kids as Owen walks in the door with some pizzas. Jess has a glass of wine ready and the five of us settle in for dinner together. I look around at my new family and feel my heart grow as they congratulate me and welcome me into their fold. We drink some wine and eat pizza and laugh. I tell them about the organization that I'll be working for, I thank them both for letting me stay with them.

"I'll start looking for a place as soon as I can," I say as I grab another slice of pizza. Owen shakes his head.

"Stay as long as you want, Sam, really. It's no bother at all. You're a big help with the twins.

I smile and bite down on the piece of pizza. I try to ignore the phone in my pocket, even though all I want to do is make sure Dean is okay. It's not that I'm not enjoying the evening, I am, it's just that a part of me is worried for him. I didn't think he'd be the type of guy to go and get wasted on a Monday afternoon.

In no time, the kids are washed and in their room for bed. Owen is reading them a story as Jess and I are in the kitchen washing up. I look over at her and smile.

"Thank you for tonight," I say. "It was so nice of you guys to do this for me."

"What, pizza and wine? Please," she laughs. "Sounds like a regular Monday night. Saves us cooking. I'm happy for you, Sam. You deserve it. The job sounds really great."

"I'm excited," I start just as the doorbell rings. We look at each other and frown as a loud knock rings out on the front door. The two of us put the dishes down and dry our hands as we head out towards the front door.

When Jess opens it, my jaw drops.

"Dean?!" I exclaim.

His eyes lift lazily up to me as he braces himself against the door frame. He's wearing a suit, but the shirt is half hanging out of his pants and his tie is loosened around his neck. His hair isn't perfectly tousled now, it's just plain messy. He's struggling to keep himself up and he opens his mouth and closes it before finally speaking.

"Sam," he slurs. "You're beautiful."

Jess glances at me and shakes her head. "Come on," she says. "Get in. Did you drive here?"

He snorts. "I'm not an idiot," he says, waving his cast in front of his face.

"Right," I say, helping Jess to support his body weight. I kick the door closed and the two of us help him to the couch. He collapses down and groans.

"Thanks. You're so beautiful," he says as he looks at me. "You're the most beautiful woman I've ever seen."

"Okay, Dean," I say, patting him on the shoulder. "You want some water?"

"No. Yeah. Okay. Yeah. Water."

Jess glances at me again and grins in disbelief. "You have

some special kind of luck with men," she whispers as we head over to the kitchen together.

"Please don't," I say with a laugh. I glance back at the couch to see him swaying back and forth. "I'm so sorry."

"It's okay, it's not your fault. Better for him to be here than out on the streets in that state. Jesus. I don't think I've seen anyone that drunk since I was in college."

By the time we get back to the living room, Dean is asleep. There's a thin line of drool dropping down his chin and his head is at an unnatural angle. Jess and I hoist his legs up and lay him down. I take his shoes off and she grabs a blanket from the end of the sofa and throws it over him. I unclasp the sling around his arm and put it on the coffee table as Jess adjust his pillows.

"I'm sorry," I whisper. "I never thought he'd show up here. I said I couldn't see him tonight."

Jess laughs. "Don't worry about it, Sam. At least you know he thinks you're beautiful."

I laugh and shake my head, look at him as he snores on Jess's couch. "Is it bad that I'm still attracted to him?"

"No, that's normal when you're smitten with someone." She looks at me with an eyebrow raised and just laughs when I stare back at her.

Smitten.

Maybe I am. I look at Dean one more time and run my finger over his cheek before following Jess back into the kitchen.

23

DEAN

THE POUNDING in my head is what wakes me up. Either that or the sun beaming down into my eyes. Maybe it's the unfamiliar voices that do it, but all I know is that when I wake up I have no idea where I am. I open my eyes slowly to see a little boy inches from my face. He has a bead of drool hanging off her chin to an incredible length and I back up in shock. The back of my head hits the end of the sofa and I wince as the throbbing in my head increases. I look around in panic, not recognizing anything around me.

The little boy giggles and reaches up to poke my face. His tiny fingers sink into my cheeks and he giggles some more.

"Who are you?" I whisper as he laughs at me. I groan and try to swing my legs off the sofa. I frown as I look down at my clothes. I'm still wearing a full suit, and my sling is folded on the coffee table beside me. I reach over to start putting it on my throbbing arm.

"He's alive!" comes a voice from behind me. There's something familiar about it, and I turn to see the mom from my last birthday party. Sam's friend. I glance back at the kid and recognize the one with the killer aim. I groan.

"Here," she says as she hands me some water and painkillers. "Have these. You were pretty drunk last night."

"Did I come here on my own?" I ask as I take the glass and pills from her. She laughs. I can't quite remember her name. Something with a J?

"You were desperate to see Samantha," she says with a grin. "You want some coffee?"

"Fuck," I say and then look at the little boy. "Sorry," I say, looking back at the woman. "I'm sorry."

"That's what Sam kept saying too," she says. "I said you'd probably have the apologies covered when you woke up. Don't worry about it. I think it's cute."

"Cute?" I ask as my eyebrows knit together. She laughs.

"Call me a hopeless romantic. What's more devoted than showing up at a girl's house completely plastered telling her how beautiful she is."

I groan and put my hand to my head. "Don't tell me, please. Don't tell me anything. Where is she?"

"She's at work. Don't worry, Dean, you weren't that bad."

"Work?" I ask, frowning. "She got a job already?"

"She's very resourceful," the woman says—Jess! That's her name. "She knew some people in town and they offered her a good job if she could start right away."

"That's great. That's really good. Fuck, and the night before she starts I show up like this. Oh my god," I groan.

Jess puts a hand on my shoulder and smiles kindly. "Don't worry about it, Dean, really. I think she was flattered."

"I'm an idiot," I say. My head is still throbbing and I reach for the glass of water again.

"Yes, but we won't hold it against you," Jess says with a

laugh. I try to smile but it feels like my face is cracking when I move. "Here, I'll grab you a towel and you can have a shower. Do you remember where your car is? I can drive you to it when you're ready. You're welcome to stay here and wait for Sam to get home, it should only be a couple hours."

"And re-live this embarrassment all over again?"

"You'll have to re-live it next time you see her anyways, she says as she walks towards a closet in the hall. "Here."

I take the towel she hands me and take a deep breath. "Thank you, Jess. You and Sam... you're both so nice. It's... I just... thanks."

Jess smiles. "It's the whole small town thing, I think." Her face settles into a serious expression as she stares at me. My heart starts beating a bit faster and she opens her mouth to speak again. Her voice is low and emotionless.

"If you break her heart, I'll break your legs. Do you understand me?"

I would laugh if she wasn't so serious. I nod slowly. "Got it."

"Good," she says, smiling again. "Bathroom is down the hall to the right. There should be soap and everything you need in there."

"Thanks. Small town kindness, hey?" I ask with a grin.

"Don't take my kindness for weakness," she responds with a smile. "Or Sam's."

I just nod and head down the hall towards the bathroom. I turn it up so hot the steam starts filling the bathroom. I strip off all my clothes and stick my arm outside the shower to save my cast from getting wet as I let the water wash over me. I groan in satisfaction as the pounding in my head dulls under the water. I wash slowly, trying to breathe some life into my heavy limbs.

By the time my shower is done I feel half-normal. I pick up my suit off the bathroom floor and put it back on, feeling fresher and more alive than I did half an hour ago. I fix my hair and take a swig of mouthwash to get rid of the furry feeling on my teeth before opening the bathroom door and stepping out.

I walk into the living room just as the front door opens and Sam walks in. She sees me and a smile breaks out across her face. The tightness in my chest loosens up and a grin starts to form on my lips.

"Hey," I say. "You're back early."

"They sent me home early after my orientation," she replies. "You look better than you did yesterday."

"That's not saying much," I laugh. "Listen, Sam, I'm sorry about all that."

She holds up a hand and kicks off her shoes before taking a step towards me. She puts her hands on either side of my face and pulls my face towards hers. I melt into her, putting my good arm around her and crushing my lips against hers. When she pulls away, her eyes are shining and she clears her throat.

"I'm sorry you lost your job. You want to talk about it?"

"Not really," I answer in a low voice. "It's bad enough I showed up here last night." All I want to do is pull her into me and kiss her again, but I hold back. "Congratulations. At least one of us is employed now."

"I'll take care of you," she says with a wink. "Might not be as glamorous as you're used to though."

"Glamorous," I say with a snort. "Wasn't too glamorous last night."

Sam puts her purse on the coffee table and starts pulling out her earrings. She glances at me and shakes her head.

"Wouldn't expect you to go off the deep end like that. I didn't know you were a drinker."

"Neither would I. I don't know what got into me. I'm sorry."

"Stop it," she says with a laugh. "You want me to drive you back to your place?" Her eyes narrow and she grins. "Was this all just an elaborate ploy to finally get me back to your apartment?"

"Is it working? If yes, then.. Yeah. I'm a mastermind."

Sam laughs. "Give me a couple minutes to get out of these work clothes and I'll bring you back."

I nod and watch as she heads down the hall. I hear her talking to Jess and I sink down on the sofa again. My heart is racing and I feel like my whole body is electrified. My hangover has disappeared and in its place is that familiar excitement in the pit of my stomach that I get whenever Sam is near.

24

SAMANTHA

"Alright, let's go!" I say as I grab my keys. Dean nods and gets up off the couch. He runs his fingers through his hair and turns around as I walk towards him.

"Thanks again," he says to Jess who followed me towards the front door. "And sorry again." She nods and smiles.

"Happens to the best of us. Glad you're feeling better."

We walk out the front door and I nod to Jess's car which is parked just outside the front door on the street.. "I guess it's my turn to open the door for you now, hey?" I laugh. I turn to look at him as I walk down the few steps towards the sidewalk. He grins and then looks beyond me and his expression falls. I turn my head to follow his gaze and my heart immediately drops to my stomach.

"Ronnie," I breathe. "What are you doing here?" I freeze, squaring my shoulders towards him as he takes a step in my direction. He holds out his hands in front of him, palms facing towards the sky.

"Sam," he says. "I'm sorry."

My blood turns to ice and a new anger starts bubbling up

inside me. How dare he! How dare he show up here, unannounced, after we've signed the divorce papers! Telling me he's *sorry*?!

"I don't want to hear it Ronnie. Go away."

"Sam, please!" he says again, taking another step towards me. Dean appears by my side.

"She said she doesn't want to see you," he growls. Ronnie's eyes swing towards Dean and his face hardens.

"Who the fuck are you?" he spits. He looks Dean up and down and puffs out his chest, balling his hands into fists. I take a step between them and try to keep my voice calm. I need to de-escalate this.

"He's my friend. Ronnie, it's over between us. You have to leave."

"Is that how it is? A lifetime of friendship and almost three years of marriage and you're just going to throw it away! And for what, for 'a friend'?" His voice is more aggressive now, and I can see that fire burning in his eyes. I take a long breath, trying to keep my own voice steady and ignore the righteous anger that's flooding through me. Before I can speak, Dean takes a step in front of me.

"She's not throwing anything away, *friend*. You're the one who fucked someone else. Now do what the lady asked and fuck right off."

Even though I know that wasn't the right thing to say, even though I know it'll only make Ronnie angry, even though I know I could have handled it better, there's still something that sparks inside me when Dean speaks up to defend me.

"What are you going to do, punch me?" Ronnie scoffs, nodding to Dean's cast. "Go ahead and try."

"I've still got one good arm, asshole," Dean growls.

"Okay, okay, okay," I say, stepping between the men. I can almost smell the testosterone in the air and I take a breath, putting my hands on Ronnie's chest. I look up at his face and wait for him to look at me. My heart breaks for the millionth time as I remember the eyes that I fell in love with, the same eyes that betrayed me.

"Ronnie, I don't want to do this. Not today, not like this." I whisper.

His shoulders slump slightly and he brings a hand to his forehead.

"I made a mistake, Sam. You need to forgive me. It was a mistake. I'm so sorry. I need you, please!" The supplication in his voice tugs at my heart and my eyes start filling with tears. Something else grows inside me at the same time. It feels like strength, or fresh air building me up and supporting my whole body. I shake my head from side to side.

"I can't, Ronnie. I just can't. Please leave." It barely comes out above a whisper. Ronnie's face contorts and twists until he doesn't look like himself anymore. He turns around and with an animalistic yell, he kicks a nearby garbage can and sends its contents flying down the sidewalk. He yells again and walks to a nearby car, getting in and speeding off down the road. Another car pulls out behind him and I watch them drive off. I frown and exchange a glance with Dean. He shrugs.

I let out a breath as my shoulders slump down. Suddenly I feel exhausted. I walk slowly to the garbage can and set it upright before bending over to pick up everything that spilled out of it. Dean appears by my side and helps me without saying a word. When we're done, he turns towards me and wraps his arm around me. I bury my head in his chest and a sob rakes through my chest as my whole body trembles. He coos and rubs my back and kisses the top of my head as I cry into his chest.

The pain in my heart eases and I pull away, wiping my eyes.

"Thanks," I say. "Sorry."

Dean laughs. "That's all I've been saying today as well."

I try to laugh but it catches in my throat. I nod to Jess's car. "Come on, let's go." Dean slides his hand down my back and we walk slowly towards the car. I get into the driver's seat and he slides into the passenger's seat as I turn the car on. I take a long, deep breath and let it all out. I swing my head over and look at Dean. He's looking at me with concern written all over his face. He reaches his hand over and stokes my cheek.

"You were great back there," he says. "I don't know how you kept your cool."

I laugh bitterly. "Lots of practice, I guess. He used to get mad a lot."

Dean stiffens and searches my face. I hate the way his eyes are boring into me and I pull my cheek away, nodding to the road and clearing my throat.

"Alright, lead the way," I say. Dean settles into his seat and we start driving. The silence is only punctuated by Dean's directions: turn left, take a right up here, left at the lights. I just nod whenever he says something, not trusting my own voice. Finally he points to a tall building.

"That's me," he says. I pull up outside and take a deep breath. I can feel him looking at me and he clears his throat. "You want to come up?"

I finally look at him again and the strength of his gaze almost knocks me over. His eyes are searching my face as if he wants to know everything about me. The ice that formed around my heart when Ronnie appeared starts to melt and I nod my head.

"Yeah," I say. "I do."

Dean smiles ever so slightly and nods his chin down once. "Cool," he says. I can help but laugh gently and feel the tension in my body start to relax a little bit more.

"Cool," I repeat.

25

DEAN

Sam looks a bit tense as the elevator dings open and I guide her down the hallway towards my door. I look at her and smile.

"Don't worry," I say as I look for my keys. "We're just going to have a drink. I'm not going to suddenly expect you to sleep with me just because you decided to come up to my apartment."

Sam's shoulders relax slightly and she smiles. She nods.

"Okay. Thanks, Dean."

I laugh as I slide the keys in the door. "I'm not an asshole, Sam. You've just had to deal with your ex acting like a toddler having a temper tantrum. I just want you to relax and feel good. I mean it." I turn to her and smile. She nods again and I tilt her chin up towards me with my finger. I lay a soft kiss on her lips and breathe in that floral scent that I've come to love over the past few days. When I pull away, Sam's smile looks a bit easier, and she lets out a sigh to relax herself.

I laugh. "Come on. What are you drinking? Wine? Whiskey? Coffee? Tell me about your new job." I step into my apartment and throw my keys onto the table by the door. I strip my jacket off and stretch my neck back and forth, heading for the fridge.

It's not until I hear Sam's gasp that I turn to look at her. Her jaw is hanging open as she looks across the room to the wall of windows. She glances back at me and shakes her head.

"You weren't kidding, the view is amazing."

"Wait until nighttime," I say as I open the fridge and grab a beer for myself. "You can see the lights of the city so clearly from up here. What are you drinking?"

"Wow," Sam says, taking a step towards the windows. She glances back at me. "I'll have whatever you're having."

I nod and pull out another beer, holding it in the crook of my broken arm to pop the cap off. Sam is opening the sliding glass doors and stepping out onto the balcony, so I bring our drinks out to join her.

"This is incredible, Dean."

"It's not bad, yeah," I reply as I lift the beer to my lips. "Easy to get used to."

Sam takes her beer and stares at me. She narrows her eyes as she searches my face, tilting her head to the side.

"Dean, how rich are you, really? I mean, all this, the cars..." Her voice trails off as she glances back at the view. I chuckle.

"I'm not struggling for money. Well, I wasn't. I never thought my own father would fire me."

Sam turns back to me and puts her hand on my arm. "I'm sorry. What happened?"

"Just family stuff," I say, not wanting to talk about it. The less I have to think about Victoria and my family, the better. Sam nods and takes a sip of her beer. The sun is starting to go down and it's giving everything a golden aura. Sam's skin looks like she's been dipped in a vat of gold, and her hair is shining like a halo around her head. I put my beer down on the table and run my fingers along her jaw to tangle them at the base of her head. She groans and takes a step closer to me, running her fingers up my chest to touch my neck.

My whole body feels electric when we kiss. The second her lips touch mine, my feet leave the ground and I'm floating in space. She wraps her fingers around my neck, her other hand still holding the bottle of beer as I pull her closer to me. I can't get enough of her. I want her closer, I want to taste her more, to feel more of her body against mine. I want to run my fingers over every inch of her and taste and kiss every bit of skin that I can find. I let my lips trail down her neck and across her collarbone as her fingers tangle into my hair. She moans and a thrill passes straight through my stomach. My cock is aching for her.

"Let's go inside," she breathes. I pull away and nod. "The couch," she says. She drops her beer next to mine and closes the sliding glass door when we step through. I sit down on the couch and groan when she swings her legs over to straddle me. Her chest is pressed against my cast, her centre next to mine. I can feel the heat between her legs radiating as my cock jumps up against my pants.

"Sam," I groan.

"What," she says, dipping her head down to kiss my earlobe, and then my neck, and then that little bit of space between my collarbones. Her lips come up to find mine again and she grinds against me as we kiss. The passion between us intensifies as she starts to unbutton my shirt, slowly at first, and then more frantically as she gets closer to my pants. She pulls the shirt away from my chest and runs her fingers up my stomach, exhaling as she watches her hand crawl up my chest.

"I've been thinking about your chest ever since the hospital parking lot," she breathes. "It feels so good to touch it."

I groan, leaning my head back against the back of the sofa. "Touch it all you want," I say. She runs her fingers up over my cast, trailing them up to my shoulders.

"You're so muscular," she says.

"I work out," I reply with a grin. Sam laughs. I run my hand down her chest and rest it against her breast. I give it a squeeze and groan as she grinds her hips into me at the same time.

"Sam," I breathe. "Are you sure about this?"

Sam's eyes flick up to mine and she bites her lip. There's a spark in her look that I've never seen before, and it sends a thrill straight to my cock. She nods her head slowly as her hand travels down my stomach to rest on top of my pants. She strokes my hard cock back and forth as I groan.

"Yeah," she finally replies. "I'm sure."

26

SAMANTHA

I don't remember the last time I was this turned on. I can feel Dean's cock through his pants and I'm literally salivating. I grind my hips slowly as my hand strokes back and forth.

This is what I've been thinking of the past few days. Every time he's been near, all I've wanted to do is be closer. I love running my fingers along his body. I love feeling the electric thrill through my veins whenever he touches me.

It feels right. As much as I didn't feel ready before, waiting has only made me want him more. The minute Ronnie appeared today, any lingering loyalty I had to him disappeared. When he threatened Dean I wanted him to leave and never come back.

Now I know that it's over between us, forever.

But in this moment, as Dean cups my breast and groans as I stroke his shaft, I don't feel sad. I feel anything but sad. I feel like my whole body is on fire and I'm finally doing what I'm supposed to be doing.

I stand up slowly and peel my shirt off, letting it drop behind me. Dean exhales as his eyes travel down to my breasts. I unclasp my bra and let it drop behind me as well. Next, I lean down and slowly unbutton his pants, sliding the zipper down inch by inch. His cock is throbbing as I open the fly of his pants and all I want to do is take it in my mouth and suck him dry.

He lifts his hips and I pull his pants down his legs as he lifts his feet to kick them aside. I hook my fingers into the waistband of his underwear and take them off he same way as his pants. I exhale as I see his cock spring free. He kicks his underwear to the side as I slide my hands up his legs, feeling the heat of his inner thighs as my hands get closer to his cock.

I wrap my fingers around his thick shaft and exhale slowly. My lips part and my heart is thumping against my ribcage as I start moving my hand up and down. Dean groans and moves his hand to my arm, stroking up and down as I work his cock.

"That feels so good, Sam," he growls. His voice is gravelly and deep and it makes the spark between my legs spread. I stand up and slide my pants down my legs in one smooth motion. Dean groans and sits up, wrapping his arm around my body and cupping my ass as he brings his face to my crotch.

Without any warning, his tongue touches my slit and my knees feel weak. I moan and fall forward, putting my hands on his shoulders to support myself. He swirls his tongue and teases my bud until the ball of desire in the pit of my stomach starts to pulse.

I lift a leg up to the sofa and Dean groans, wrapping his lips around my bud to suck and lick and taste me. He moves his hand from my ass and slides his fingers inside me. I whimper, gripping his shoulder and grinding my face towards him. His fingers move in tandem with his mouth until I can feel the wetness gushing out of me. He groans as his tongue keeps exploring my slit and flicking over my bud until I feel like I'm going to fall over.

"Stop, stop," I pant, taking a step back. He looks up at me, lips glistening.

"You okay?"

"I'm fine. Fuck. I'm better than fine. I was about to fall over," I pant, pushing his shoulders back as I kneel on the sofa. I move my hand down his stomach and grab his cock. The precum is beading on the tip as I wrap my hand around him. I stroke it gently, moving my hips until the tip of his cock is sliding back and forth along my slit. He lets out a long, low groan and I close my eyes to enjoy the sensation of his cock in my hand.

I can't take it anymore. It's too much. I want him too badly, and I can't think about anything except his pulsing cock and my waiting, aching body.

I close my eyes and sit down to take the length of him in one smooth motion. My head falls back as my body stretches to accept him. I hear myself moan as he enters me for the first time. When our hips connect, I take a moment to gasp and open my eyes. He's staring at me, mouth open and eyes bright as his hand moves to grab my ass. I put my hands on his chest, avoiding his cast as I pant. I'm still not moving.

"That feels so good," I breathe.

"I know," he growls.

With that, I start grinding my hips back and forth on top of him. I whimper as my body opens for him and he starts to thrust his hips towards me. He's so deep inside me that it feels like my insides are being rearranged. My head falls back and my mouth opens as I start grinding my hips on him harder.

I dig my fingers into his chest and start moving my hips up and down, bouncing on his cock as he grips my ass. He slams his cock back up into me. He's grunting and moaning in the sexiest way I've ever heard. The power of his thrusts is making my tits bounce up and down and I feel like all I can do is hang on.

My orgasm starts as a ball of flames in the pit of my stomach, and with every thrust it gets hotter and heavier until I can't think of anything except his cock entering me again and again and again. His fingers sink into my ass and he grunts again as he slams his cock inside me.

The release is unreal. I've never had an orgasm like this before. I've never been fucked like this before. It feels like my walls are gushing and my body is being pulled apart in every direction. I don't realize I'm screaming until a few seconds later. The fire in my veins flows through my body in wave after wave of pleasure.

Dean doesn't stop driving his cock into me and I don't stop coming. Hs cock gets ever harder and his whole body tenses. He moans and I look down to see the sinews of his neck bulging as his cock pulses inside me. I gasp as I feel him fill me with his seed just as my own orgasm is dying down.

Finally, he opens his eyes and looks up at me. We're both panting and covered in a thin sheen of sweat. I can't say anything, I can't think anything, I can't do anything except stay completely still and try to breathe.

"Whoa," Dean says between breaths.

"Yeah," I manage to respond. I close my eyes and breathe, still feeling my walls contracting around his throbbing cock. "Whoa."

27

DEAN

Sam peels herself up off the couch and I point her towards the bathroom.

"Use the bathroom through my bedroom. It has a shower and clean towels." She smiles and lays a soft kiss on my lips before walking away. I lean back on the sofa and let out a long breath, laying my head back and closing my eyes. I can't believe that just happened. It's exactly what I imagined the other night, exactly what I fantasized about. The reality was so much better than my mind. I sigh again. I'm not ready to move yet.

It feels like no time goes by when Sam slides against me and curls up against my shoulder. I open my eyes and look over at her. I start chuckling. She's batting her eyelashes at me and wearing the big red nose from my clown costume.

"You think I'm sexy?" she purrs, wagging the nose back and forth.

I laugh. "Incredibly sexy, yes."

She pulls the nose off and looks at it, smiling. "I still can't believe I've had sex with a clown."

"Is that all I am to you? Just a clown?" I tease.

She crinkles her nose and grins. "Children's entertainer, Dean, please. Have some self respect."

I laugh and stretch my arm out around her shoulders. She leans into my chest and runs her fingers over my other shoulder and down my cast.

"Is it sore?" she asks, brushing my fingers and running her hand back up towards my shoulder.

"A bit, I guess, now that you mention it. I forgot about it for a while there," I chuckle. "I was distracted."

Sam grins and then lifts her head to look at me. "Is it just me, or was that sex *really* hot? Like, unusually hot."

"It was great, that's what it was," I reply as I dip my lips down to hers. "You're an animal."

She laughs and purrs, clawing her hand towards me like a cat. I laugh and Sam gets up, pulling on her underwear and shirt. She walks outside and grabs our forgotten beers, handing me one of them and taking a long sip of her own. I do the same, and after a pause she looks at me and cocks her head to the side.

"So why did you get fired?"

I lift my eyes to hers, trying to gauge the seriousness of her question. My heart starts beating a little bit harder as I try to think of what to say. I could tell her the truth, but what kind of family would she think I have? I don't want her to think I'm just another rich kid with rich kid problems and sociopathic parents. I don't want her to think that I'm only interested in her for sex and I'll end up just leaving her for someone of my parent's choosing. If I'm honest, I don't want to think about my family at all. I just want to enjoy my time with her.

I clear my throat. "I wouldn't do something my parents

asked me to do," I answer, knowing that I haven't answered her question at all.

She nods slowly. "Was it work related?" I frown and she continues. "The thing they asked you to do, was it work related?"

"Not exactly," I answer. I open my mouth to elaborate but something stops me and I close it again. She nods.

"I didn't mean to pry," she says.

"It's fine. I just... I just don't want to talk about it."

The corner of her lips starts curling upwards ever so slightly. She points her beer bottle at me and tilts her head to the side. "You know what's way better than talking about it?"

"What's that," I answer as the smile starts spreading across my face.

"Drinking yourself stupid, showing up at my house, and passing out on my couch," she replies as her grin widens. She raises her eyebrows and takes a sip of beer and I can't help but laugh.

"Alright, alright. I deserved that," I laugh. She sits down beside me and chuckles as she sits back on the sofa.

"I don't know whether to be flattered or disgusted," she says as she takes another sip.

"Well, I hope you aren't disgusted with me," I answer, leaning over to kiss her lips. She smiles.

"Definitely not."

She runs her fingers along my jaw and lays a tender kiss on my lips. A soft moan escapes her and I wrap my good arm around her body, pulling her closer. Her hand tangles into my hair and our lips crush together. I breathe in deeply and let her smell and her heat and her body envelop me completely.

Finally, she pulls away and looks at me with her eyes shining brightly. She smiles and then sighs.

"I should probably head back," she sighs.

"You don't want to stay? You don't have to leave. We could have dinner, you can go tomorrow morning."

She shakes her head slowly. "It's my second day at work tomorrow, I want to make sure I'm there on time. Plus, I have Jess's car and she probably wouldn't be too happy if I kept it all night."

I chuckle. "Fair enough."

"You need me to drive you to your car? You came by taxi last night."

"No, it's okay, I never took it out yesterday. Thanks though," I reply with a smile. I run my finger along her cheek and tuck a strand of hair behind her ear. "You're always thinking of me. Thank you."

She grins. "That's just how I am. Don't flatter yourself,"

I laugh and throw my hand up. She smiles again and kisses me one more time before standing up. I watch her pull on her clothes before leaning over to grab my jocks. I pull them on with one hand as Sam grabs her purse. She turns towards me and wraps her arms around my neck.

"I'll be pretty busy with work, but maybe we could hang out this weekend?"

"Can't wait," I say. "I'm free anyways, so just let me know. I've got nowhere to be," I say with a wry smile. "Unemployment has its perks."

She laughs and nods before turning towards the door. She opens it and turns around to take one last look at me before slipping out. I sigh and lock the door behind her, leaning my head against the door and closing my eyes for a moment.

Slowly, I turn around and swing my eyes across my apartment. My pants are still in a heap by the sofa, and our beer bottles are on the coffee table. The lights of the city are starting to twinkle outside the window as the sun goes down and I sigh again.

It feels lonelier than it's ever felt in here. I know that people would kill for an apartment like this, but I can't help but wonder what's the point of having it if I've got no one to share it with. I wander to the fridge and grab another beer, looking at the green bottle for a second before cracking it open. This is my last one tonight, because I'm definitely not doing what I did yesterday.

I sit down on the couch and flick on the TV. I can't wait for the weekend and I don't even have a job. I just want to see her again.

28

SAMANTHA

I'M HUMMING to myself as I press the elevator button and head down to the ground floor. My body is still pulsing from my orgasm and I can taste Dean's kiss on my lips. I can't help but smile to myself as the doors ding open and I take a step out.

"Oops! Sorry," I say to an older woman as she tries to step in at the same time. My smile fades as she frowns at me. She doesn't move, so I have to side-step and walk around her to get out of the elevator. I look over my shoulder to see her pressing a button just as the elevator doors close. I turn back towards the front door and frown. Something about her seemed familiar, but I don't know what.

She was impeccably dressed in a matching pantsuit, with her hair pulled back in a low bun. She had expensive-looking jewelry that was simple yet elegant.

In a word, she looked rich.

I shake my head and start walking towards the front door. I still think I'm in Lexington, where I know everyone and their dog. I'm in New York City now, and I know no one. Of course I didn't know that woman. And if she lives in the building, of course she would be rich. I can't imagine anybody in the middle class living in this place.

Still, the way her face soured when we almost stepped into each other made me uneasy. I take a deep breath and walk out the automatic sliding doors and find Jess's car. By the time I slide into the driver's seat, the woman is out of my mind.

I take my time going back to Jess's place, noticing all the shops and people and houses along the way. It really is the city that never sleeps. Every day I see things I've never seen before. I pull up outside Jess's house and sigh.

I wish I didn't have to leave. I've only just met Dean and I want to spend more time with him. I can't make any sense of him—he's like a bunch of opposites stuck together. An investment banker who moonlights as a clown for children's parties, a billionaire's son who is completely down to earth, a man who's been through heartbreak who seems to wear his heart on his sleeve.

I smile as I think of the way he tucked my hair behind my ear earlier. His touch was so tender and it sent a shiver through my body. I get out of the car and head up towards the front door. There's a small package on the front step and I bend over to pick it up. I frown as I see my name scrawled across the top of it.

I give the package a light shake and turn it over. It's a small box, about the size of a pencil case. It's wrapped in brown paper with '*SAM*' scrawled across the top in black sharpie. It feels light. I read my name a few times and give it a shake, but I can't feel anything. The unease I felt earlier when I ran into that woman returns to the pit of my stomach. I tuck the package under my arm and find my keys to go inside.

As soon as I step inside, I hear the pitter-patter of tiny feet running towards me. I kneel down and spread my arms as two toddlers collide with me. I laugh and wrap them both into a hug. Jess isn't far behind, chasing after them as usual. I lift them up and they giggle as I carry them towards the living room.

"You look happy!" Jess exclaims. She picks up the package that I dropped when the twins ran towards me and follows me to the living room. "You were gone a while, I was starting to get worried."

"You were not," I say as I shoot a glance her way. She laughs and shakes her head.

"No, I wasn't. I thought you might be enjoying yourself," she says as she wiggles her eyebrows. I roll my eyes and turn to Michelle, tickling her until she's giggling and writhing on the floor. Matt runs to protect his sister and starts scrunching his hands under my armpits to try to tickle me too. I pretend to laugh and fall over and pretty soon both kids are on top of me attacking me with tickles. I laugh and finally peel them off me to stand up.

"He's a nice guy," I finally answer.

"Mm-hmm," Jess replies, lifting an eyebrow slightly. My cheeks flush as she holds out the package. "What's this?"

"I'm not sure, it was by the front door." I turn it over again and look up at Jess. "Ronnie showed up earlier."

"What?"

"Yeah, just as I was leaving. He made a scene and then left. I wonder…". My voice trails off as I stare at the package in my hands. Jess's hand appears on my forearm.

"Sam," she says. Her voice is soft and her eyes are full of concern. "You don't have to open it. It doesn't matter what it is. If he keeps showing up you could charge him with harassment. You don't have to put up with this." She stands up a bit straighter and shakes his head. "I can't believe he showed up here! How did he get my address?!"

"He must have asked my mom," I reply as I shake my head. I put the package on a shelf and take a deep breath. "I won't open it tonight. I feel too good."

"Exactly," Jess says. "Enjoy this feeling. Enjoy your freedom and enjoy your glorious post-orgasmic glow."

"Jess!" I exclaim, my cheeks flushing even more. She just laughs and waves a hand in front of her face.

"Did you think I couldn't tell?"

I bite my lip and start laughing. Just then, the twins appear beside me and latch on to each of my legs. I laugh and start walking across the living room as they hold on, giggling the whole way. Jess shakes her head.

"They love you," she says with a smile. "You're great with kids."

I sigh and ruffle Matt's hair. "I was hoping to have one of my own by now," I admit. My lips purse together and I lift my eyes up to Jess. "Looks like that'll have to wait."

"You never know," she says with a grin. "You're moving pretty fast with this clown of yours."

I blush again and shake my head. "Not that fast."

Jess laughs. "Come on," she says. "I need to put those two in the bath. There's some spaghetti on the stove if you're hungry."

"Thanks," I say, handing off the twins to her waiting arms. I watch her walk down the halls and talk to her children and I feel something in the pit of my stomach. Owen appears and gives me a wave before following her to the bathroom. They have such a nice life together. Two beautiful kids, a supportive, loving husband—am I jealous of Jess? I thought I had what she has, but it turns out all I had was betrayal and heartbreak.

My eyes flick to the brown paper package on the shelf and I shake my head. I walk to the kitchen and grab a bowl. My stomach growls in appreciation as I start spooning spaghetti into my dish.

My phone buzzes and I glance at the screen. A smile forms on my lips and the jealousy I felt a few minutes ago disappears. Dean's name flashes on the screen.

Dean: I had a good time tonight.

I grin and type out my answer, holding my phone to my chest for a second as I remember the evening I just had. Life isn't so bad, and Jess is right. Maybe my happily-ever-after isn't so far away after all.

29

DEAN

It feels like only a minute or two since Sam left when a knock comes on the door. I glance around the apartment as I walk towards the front door, wondering if she forgot something. I don't see anything of hers and I grab the door handle with a grin across my face. I open the door, ready to see Sam's smiling face.

"Mom!" I exclaim. "What are you doing here?"

"Good to see you too, Dean," she says sarcastically, her eyes traveling down to my underwear. "Is that a way to greet your own mother?"

"What are you doing here?" I ask again. My whole body is tense as we stare at each other across the doorway.

"You're not going to invite me in?" she replies. I pause for a moment before stepping aside. My mother walks into my apartment. I close the door and walk over to my discarded pants and pull them on, shimmying from side to side as I pull them up with one hand.

"Your father told me what happened yesterday," she says as she sits on the edge of a chair, crossing her legs and folding her hands on top of her knee. Everything about her is perfectly manicured, with not a single hair out of place. All her movements are deliberate and she looks around the room with a hint of disgust on her face.

I grunt in response and grab the empty beer bottles from the coffee table to throw them out.

"Won't you be reasonable, Dean? Your father is willing to take you back in at work if you just listen to what he has to say."

"Reasonable?!" I exclaim as I drop the bottles in the garbage. "You want me to be reasonable?! I would say it's reasonable to break up with someone who cheated on you. Wouldn't you?"

My mother waves a hand dismissively and huffs. "You talk as if marriage is about love, Dean. This is so much bigger than that. We've had this planned since you were a child."

"Did you ever consider what I might want? Maybe I don't want to go into politics, maybe I do want to marry for love. What about that? Maybe I don't want a wife who sleeps with other men in our own bed."

"She made a mistake, Dean," my mother says. "She shouldn't have brought someone else back to your place."

"But if she'd done it somewhere else it would be okay?" I spit back. "What if it had been me? What if it had been me who had cheated? How would *her* family react? Would the deal still be on?"

"You'd never do that, son, I know you wouldn't."

"That's not the point, mom. The point is that if it had been me, they would be outraged and the deal would be off. There's probably some morality clause that excuses us from the deal in this situation, isn't there? But you won't use it because you're so fucking power hungry that you'd ignore what I actually want."

My mother's eyes narrow and her voice is low when she speaks.

"You're forgetting that 'what you want' is only possible because of what your father and I sacrificed. Have some respect," she spits the last word at me and then pats the sides of her head, smoothing her perfect hair back. "Dean," she starts again, a bit more softly, "This is bigger than you. There are arrangements that can be made for marriages like this to work. Your father and I..."

"I don't want to hear about your fucked up marriage, mother. Have you ever considered that I don't want what you have? Maybe it isn't worth it to me!"

My mother laughs. She sweeps her arm across the room and raises an eyebrow. "All this isn't worth it? That nice black Bentley isn't worth it? Those credit cards aren't worth it? Let me teach you something, Dean," she snarls as she gets up off the seat. She takes a step towards me and pokes her long fingernail into my chest. "You'll see how *worth it* it is. You're cut off."

I open my mouth and close it again, frowning. "Cut off? What do you mean?"

"I mean it's time to chop these apron strings, my dear son," she says with a cruel smile. "No more trust fund. No more mommy and daddy. No more credit cards from our line of credit. Nothing. If you won't be part of the family business and the family dynasty, then you are on your own. I'm giving you three months, Dean. After three months you'll be ready to come back to the family."

She pulls her hand back and turns on her heels, heading for the front door. I watch her walk away and watch the door swing shut. It's not until I hear the elevator ding down the hall that I'm pulled out of my stupor. I shuffle to the front door in a daze and slide the lock closed before turning around in my apartment.

Cut off.

I've always felt independent, but she's right. Everything is from the business accounts. The car, the apartments, the credit cards... none of it is mine. I have some savings, sure, but that won't keep me going long. I put a hand to my head and let out a breath. I haven't even realized how dependent I am on my parents until right now.

I'm being cut off.

Once the shock starts to wear off, anger starts curling around my stomach. My own mother is sucking me dry, cutting me off just because I won't play along with their little power play! My parents don't respect me as a person, or care how I feel. They only want their own fucking master plan to come to fruition.

"Fuck!" I yell, slamming my hand down on the counter. My heart is thumping in my chest and I take a few deep breaths, trying to figure out what I'll do. I walk back and forth a few times and finally head out to the balcony. The cold night air fills my lungs and I take a deep breath, letting it cool my anger ever so slightly. I'm still shirtless, and within a few seconds, goosebumps start forming on my skin. I shiver, but I don't go inside. The chill feels good and it helps to clear my head.

They may be cutting me off but that doesn't mean I'm destitute. I have money, I have skills, I have contacts. I can find work for another firm and actually be independent for once. I can be my own man and not rely on my parent's money to support me.

As much as I'm hurt by my parent's indifference, and as scared as I am about being on my own, there's a sense of excitement that starts budding in the pit of my stomach. It's about time I was my own man. Maybe my mother was right. It's time to cut the apron strings.

30

SAMANTHA

THE DAYS DRAG on until the weekend. Finally, it's Friday and I pack an extra pair of underwear, deodorant, and a toothbrush in my purse. *Just in case,* I tell myself as my heart skips a beat. I walk out of my room and Jess winks at me.

"Have fun," she says.

"I will," I answer and kiss the kids' heads. "I'll see you later."

I walk towards the front door and my eye catches the little brown box sitting on the shelf, exactly where I left it earlier this week. I pause, staring at it, and then shake my head. Not tonight. I don't want to know what Ronnie sent me. I already know it would only upset me.

I head out to the waiting cab and give him the address of the restaurant. We pull up outside and I frown.

"Are you sure this is it?" I ask.

"This is Emilio's on East 104th," he replies in a gruff voice. I nod and pay him before stepping out. It's not that it isn't nice, it's just that compared to the glamour of our last date, it's a bit more understated. Who am I kidding, it looks completely run down. The paint is peeling and the sign looks like it's about a hundred years old. If there wasn't a light shining inside, I could have mistaken the restaurant for an abandoned building. I shake my head and smile. Even a couple dates in, I'm already expecting to be spoiled. I chuckle. I need to keep an open mind and be myself.

I head towards the restaurant door when I hear my name.

"Sam!" Dean is jogging down the street, one arm stretched above his head. He still has his sling on, and he's holding his arm tight to his chest. My heart grows a few sizes as he gets closer. He wraps his arm around me and pulls me in for a kiss.

"Mmm," he says. "You taste minty!"

I laugh. "I wanted to be prepared."

Dean smiles and nods to the restaurant. "I know it's a bit different from last time, but I know the owner and this is the best Italian food in Manhattan outside of Little Italy."

"It looks great," I say. "More my style."

"Good," he says. "Plus, I got fired. I'm on a budget now," he laughs.

"Well don't stretch yourself too thin," I grin. "Dinner's on me tonight."

He opens the door and motions me through with a sweeping motion. I step through and we're immediately greeted by a short bald man. He's wider than he is tall and has bright red ruddy cheeks. He's wearing a white apron and has a thick grey mustache.

"Mister Dean!" He calls out. His eyes swing over to me and he brings his hand to his heart and bows. I smile. "This must be your beautiful date. Please," he says, extending a hand. I slip mine into his and smile as he leans over to kiss my hand. I giggle as his mustache tickles my hand and glance up at Dean. He shakes his head.

"Emilio, keep this up and I'll be leaving here alone. You'll steal her off me!"

"No, no, no! Come!" He motions us over to a table near the front of the restaurant. It's beautifully set, with a rich white tablecloth and a candle flickering in the middle. There's a single daisy in a simple vase, and red cloth napkins folded into an elaborate triangle on the plates. Emilio pulls out my chair and another waiter appears with wine. I grin at Dean.

"What did I tell you," he says. "What are we having tonight, Emilio?"

"Tonight we have a delicious meal planned," he starts. For the next couple minutes, he's rattling off dishes and ingredients and wine pairings and I can hardly keep up. All I know is that it sounds delicious. Dean thanks him and he promises to check in with us again once we have our food. Dean smiles at me.

"I always have Emilio prepare a set menu when I come here. I hope you don't mind."

"Not at all," I reply with a smile. My heart is beating in my chest and I put my hand across the table. Dean places his palm over mine and we stare at each other for a few moments.

I'm so happy right now. I feel so lucky! Coming to New York was the best decision I ever made. I lose myself in Dean's eyes and all thoughts of Ronnie, the divorce, and that little brown box evaporate from my mind.

We have another spectacular meal, and after many thank you's and promises to come back, we leave Emilio and the staff behind. I put a hand to my stomach as I hook my other arm around Dean's.

"That was amazing, but I feel like I could roll home."

"It's a lot of food," Dean laughs. "Come on, Central Park is right here. Let's go for a walk."

It feels less like a walk and more like I'm floating through space. He interlaces his fingers into mine and I lean my head against his shoulder as we walk and talk and laugh. I don't remember the last time I felt this good. I don't know if it's the wine, or Dean, or the beautiful starry night, but everything feels so perfect.

We walk wherever our feet take us, and soon Dean is hailing a cab and giving his address. My heart starts beating and I squeeze his hand, feeling the heat growing at the meeting of my legs. Dean looks down at me and smiles. His face drops and he looks at his cast, sighing.

"I can't wait to get this thing off so I can fuck you properly," he growls. My heart jumps and my centre blossoms with heat at his words. I can feel my cheeks flushing.

"Not too long," I manage to reply. He smiles just as the cab pulls up outside his place. By the time we're in the elevator, we're clawing at each other's clothes, crushing our lips together, tangling our fingers into each other's hair.

"I don't think you need two hands," I say as the elevator opens. "You're doing pretty well with just one."

Dean grins and nods to his door. "Let's go."

31

DEAN

Sam's body has so many little secrets that I love discovering. There's the freckles across her nose and the thousands of freckles that scatter across her chest. She has a mole on her left hip that I kiss gently, and a little patch of skin on her right thigh that's impossibly soft. Every curve, every freckle, every inch of skin feels like it was made for me to worship. I run my hand all over her body as she watches me and I wish I could use both hands. I want to know her body as well as I know my own.

I've been dreaming of her taste ever since the first night, and I finally get to taste her again. We make love again and again, writhing and grinding and touching and kissing and coming until all my energy is spent. I sigh. All I can do is lay back and trail my finger back and forth along her side. She shivers and purrs against me.

"I had such a good time tonight," she says.

"Me too. When do you have to work next?" I ask.

She lifts her head slightly and frowns at me. "Not till Monday," she answer. "Why?"

"Stay with me," I whisper. I'm not ready to let her go, not ready to watch her walk out the door. A smile breaks across her face and she nods.

"Okay."

She puts her head back on my shoulder and I feel like it was made for her. I run my finger over and back across her body and she shivers again before her breath deepens and I know she's asleep. I'm not far behind, falling into the deepest and most peaceful sleep I've had in months.

We spend the weekend just like that—eating and walking and talking and fucking over and over and over. I'm in heaven. I keep exploring her body and finding new things to love about it, and she keeps exploring mine. Sunday night comes too soon, and despite my protests, Sam kisses me goodbye.

"I'll call you tomorrow," she says.

"I wish you worked closer to here," I say with a grin. "It's so much better when you're around."

"Me too," she smiles. With one more kiss, she walks out the door and heads home. I sigh, locking the door behind her and once again turning around to my cold, empty apartment.

I head to my bedroom and flop down onto the bed. I should feel good, I know I should. I got a call last week from another firm who's willing to give me an interview, I've spent the weekend with a gorgeous woman, and I'm finally living my life as my own man.

I should be happy, and I am! I am happy. I just can't shake the feeling that it isn't right. I don't like fighting with my parents and the cruelty in my mother's face when she left surprised me. I find it hard to believe that she would let me go so easily, when their entire future in politics relied on my marriage to Victoria.

With a deep breath, I try to put the thoughts behind me. I lay down in bed and I can still smell Sam's perfume on the pillow. I smile and inhale deeply, already looking forward to seeing her again.

THE NEXT FEW weeks go by just like that. I end up finding a job at a rival firm and slip into a new routine at work. Sam and I see each other whenever we can, and she sleeps over on the weekends and a couple nights a week. My arm heals, and Sam comes with me to get the cast off. It's easy, and without me even knowing when it happens, I realize I'm happy. I wake up one Sunday morning and turn to see Sam. She's snoring lightly, her brown hair across the pillow like a brush stroke and her face completely peaceful as she sleeps. I take a finger and run it gently over her cheek, smiling as she shivers.

Her eyes flutter open.

"Hey," she murmurs.

"Hey," I answer. "Didn't mean to wake you."

"It's okay. How's the arm feeling today?"

I close and open my fist a few times and shrug. "A bit stiff but it's okay. I'll do the exercises the doctor gave me and it should loosen right up." She nods and rolls onto her back, stretching her arms overhead. I drag my eyes over her body as she groans. She turns around suddenly, holding a hand to her mouth. She sits up and swings her legs over the edge of the bed.

"What's wrong?" I say, concerned.

She shakes her head and slowly lowers her hand. "It's

nothing. Thought I might have to run to the bathroom but I think I'm safe."

"You should really get that checked out, Sam. Is it the nausea again?"

She nods her head and takes a deep breath. "It usually passes within a couple minutes. I don't want to go to the doctor for something so small."

I shake my head and run my hand over her stomach. "It's not small, Sam. I'll take you. You could have a stomach bug or something."

She nods slowly and then turns to me suddenly. "Oh! I forgot to say on Friday, I spoke to Margaret. She agreed to let you come and do a show for the kids. Can you come tomorrow night?"

"Sure," I answer. "I'll let Pat know. Did she agree to the partnership with him?"

"She said we could have you there for an afternoon or two and see how the kids react. She liked the idea of the balloon animal lessons and juggling lessons."

I grin. "Awesome. Pat's gonna be over the moon, he's been looking to expand the non-profit business of it into something like this for years."

I wrap my arm around her and pull her in for a kiss. I nuzzle my head into her body and she giggles when I kiss her and blow air over her neck. She wraps her legs around me and I lift my head to see that look in her eye—that look that makes me hard every time I see it.

"I love waking up next to you," I say. Sam's eyes soften and a smile tugs at her lips. She nods.

"Me too," she whispers.

"Stay tonight. Don't go to work tomorrow," I say.

Sam smiles. "I can't, you know I can't. I have to leave in a couple hours."

"The past couple months…" I start. She holds up a hand and puts it over my lips.

"I know. I didn't think I could be this happy so soon after the divorce." I smile and bring my lips to hers. We kiss softly and my cock throbs between my legs. She feels it and wriggles her body, laughing and wiggling her eyebrows.

"What do we have here?" she purrs. I don't even have time to answer. Our bodies are already intertwined and connected and once again I make love to the most incredible woman I've ever known.

32

SAMANTHA

After a fitful sleep at Jess's house, I wake up and rush to the bathroom. For the past couple weeks, every time I wake up I have the worst nausea I've ever felt. After emptying my stomach into the toilet bowl, I take a deep breath and flush the toilet before brushing my teeth. When I open the door, Jess is standing there with her arms crossed and her best mom face on. She raises an eyebrow and looks me up and down.

"Get your shoes on, we're going to the doctor."

"What! No, it's okay. Jess, I'm fine. It's just a stomach bug or something."

"Stomach bugs don't last two weeks. Come one. Owen!" she calls out. He answers from the bedroom. "Watch the twins, I'm taking Sam to the doctor."

"Okay!" comes the answer. She tuns to me and nods her head.

"Come on."

There's no arguing with that tone of voice, so I nod and

get my shoes and purse. I check my phone, expecting to see something from Dean.

"That's weird," I say as I join Jess by the front door. "Dean is supposed to come to the organization today and do a clown show but he hasn't messaged me. Usually he'd send me something in the morning."

"Maybe he's busy," she says as we walk out to the car. When we're in it, Jess turns it on but doesn't drive off. She turns to me and takes a deep breath.

"When's the last time you got your period?"

I frown at the question. She doesn't think that I'm....?

"I'm on the pill," I say. She nods slowly.

"And you've been taking it every day?"

I chew my lip and stare at my hands. "Well, there was a bit of a mix-up a few weeks ago and I forgot for a couple days. But I took the ones I missed! I spotted a bit but then everything is back to normal. I'm supposed to be on the sugar pills next week."

She nods slowly. "How many days did you miss?"

"Jess, I'm not pregnant. I'm on the pill!"

I finally lift my eyes back up to her and her brows are drawn together. She shakes her head. "I told you to be careful, Sam. I warned you."

"I'm not pregnant!" I repeat. "And please don't say 'I told you so.' I can't deal with that right now."

She nods. "You're right, I'm sorry. Let's just go to the doctor and see what they say. I'm here for you."

My throat tightens and I nod in response. We drive in silence and my mind starts clouding with a hurricane of thoughts.

Pregnant?

I can't be. I'm not pregnant. I'm on the pill! How could I be pregnant. Sure, I got a bit sloppy taking it when I was going back and forth between her place and Dean's. I forgot my pack in my room and went without for a couple days. But that wouldn't cause pregnancy... would it?

My doubts only increase as we make it to the clinic's waiting room. Jess sits with me and thumbs through a magazine as I check my phone again. Still nothing from Dean, even after I sent him a text. He hasn't even been online since last night.

I sigh just as another patient walks in with a cup of coffee. The smell hits my nose and I feel my stomach heave. I run to the bathroom and for the second time this morning, I get to know the toilet bowl more intimately than I want to. When I walk back out, the doctor is calling my name.

The rest of the appointment is a blur. From the moment the doctor says 'pregnant', I cease to hear anything except my own heartbeat in my ears. I don't see anything except the stark white walls and that picture of the digestive system that every doctor seems to have in their office.

I sign something, and I leave her office with some pamphlets. Jess says something to me and I think I have a follow-up appointment, but to be honest I can't make any sense of it. It's like I don't speak English anymore, or I've suddenly lost the ability to understand anything that's said. Jess takes me by the arm and guides me back to her car, all the while saying things that I don't understand. They sound vaguely comforting, but they bring me no comfort.

I stare straight ahead as we drive back and finally Jess stops talking. My eyes shift down to the pamphlets in my hands. I look at the pictures of smiling expectant mothers and try to read the words but they blur together. When we pull up to the house, I get out of the car mechanically and make it to my bedroom. I sit on the edge of the bed and stare at the wall for a moment, or maybe longer. I don't know.

It's not until Jess knocks on the door frame that I'm snapped out of my daze. I look over at her and she hands me a steaming mug of tea.

"You okay?"

I nod. "I think so. I mean. I don't know. Jess…"

"I won't say 'I told you so,'" she says with a smile as she sits down beside me. She wraps an arm around my shoulder and squeezes me into her. "Everything is going to be okay. Whatever you decide to do, it'll be okay."

"What do you mean, 'whatever I decide to do'?" I look over at her and see the pain in her eyes. Her eyebrows knit together and she takes a deep breath.

"With the baby," she says, almost in a whisper.

It takes a few seconds for me to understand what she means. Once it sinks in, I sit up a bit straighter and blurt out the first thing that comes to mind.

"I'm keeping it," I say, almost too loudly in the small room. She squeezes my shoulder gently and nods.

"Okay."

She doesn't need to say anything else. Suddenly I'm shaking, and the tears are starting to fall down my cheeks. She squeezes me close and I let myself melt into her, letting her rock me back and forth and making comforting noises as I sob on her shoulder. It's not until I feel a small hand on my knee that I open my eyes to see Michelle staring up at me.

Her tiny face is filled with concern, and she spreads her arms towards me. I laugh through my tears and pick her up. She places a big, sloppy, two-year-old kiss on my cheek and pats my head. I laugh again as Jess chuckles and strokes Michelles hair.

"You're going to have a little cousin soon. Auntie Sam is having a baby," I say to her. She looks at me with those bright blue intelligent eyes and I turn to Jess. "I swear she understands everything we say."

Jess laughs. "She does. So will yours."

A thrill passes through my stomach and I move my hand across my abdomen. I look down and take a deep breath. I'm going to be a mother. The next thought makes me stiffen and I struggle to keep my breath steady.

How am I going to tell Dean?

33

SAMANTHA

I CHECK my watch and glance at the door. My boss, Margaret, is throwing me a look and raising her eyebrow and I take a deep breath. I was a few minutes late to work and now Dean is as well. It's not looking good.

"Come on, Dean, where are you?" I say under my breath. He's late, and it took a lot of convincing to get Margaret to agree to have him do a clown show for the kids at the after-school program.

Finally, the door bursts open and dozens of heads turn towards the door. Dean appears in full costume, bursting through the door and pretending to fall over. He does a full flip and lands on his feet as the room full of kids burst into laughter. A few of them get up and run to him and I get to watch him do what I saw the very first day we met.

It's one of his best performances, and I slide over to Margaret whose face softens a little bit.

"He's good, right?" I say as Dean starts his balloon animal bit. Margaret's face looks like it's fighting not to smile. She nods once.

"He's not bad. We'll see how it goes."

With that, she turns to a nearby child and I look at Dean. I give him a subtle thumbs up and he winks at me before turning back to the kids. I sit back and start watching the show. A soft smile plays on my lips as I watch him captivate the children's attention and make them laugh and giggle with every move. Maybe everything will be okay. He obviously loves kids, maybe he'll want to have one of his own.

I'm so engrossed that I almost jump when Margaret touches me on the shoulder.

"Someone's here to see you," she says, nodding to the door. I frown and nod at her before heading towards the front door. For some reason, my heart starts beating a bit harder as I push the door open and glance down the hallway.

That's when I see her.

A chill runs down my spine as she turns to face me. She's taller than I am, and in her six-inch heels she towers over me. She's wearing a tight, fitted grey dress with a sharp white blazer. Her black hair is silky and straight, and it sways when she turns towards me. Her heels clack on the floor when she steps in my direction, and she stretches her hand out to shake mine.

When our palms touch, I have to stop myself from recoiling. Something in her eyes fills me with a deep sense of unease. Her lips curl into a smile that seems jarring against her other features, like her face wasn't meant to smile.

"Samantha," she says. "So nice to finally meet you."

"Do we know each other?" I ask, already knowing the answer. She laughs melodically and shakes her head. Her long hair sways with every movement and her eyes drill into me.

"You should stay away from him," she says slowly. My

heart starts thumping and my chest feels hollow. I stand my ground and take a slow breath, trying to understand what she's saying.

"Who?"

"Your new boyfriend," she replies with venom. "You should stay away from him. He isn't what he seems, and he's just going to break your precious little heart."

"What do you know? Who the fuck are you?" I ask, squaring my shoulders. I feel silly in my no-nonsense shoes, hair pulled into a messy bun as she stands up straighter and towers over me, exuding wealth and poise. She lifts an eyebrow and almost snarls at me.

"In the end, he'll choose his family. Wealthy people always do. We're not like the rest of you."

I almost choke as I try to respond. "The rest of us?!" She shrugs.

"Don't say I didn't warn you."

"Who are you?"

Instead of answering, she turns around and walks out of the building. I watch her hips sway from side to side, and see her slide on a pair of sunglasses as she pushes the door open. Relief washes over me as soon as she leaves the building and I turn back to the main room. The kids start flowing out as I walk back in, calling out goodbyes and see-you-tomorrows as they rush past. My tense body starts to relax and I head back inside.

Margaret and Dean are talking, and she starts laughing. I look at Dean and shake my head. Only he would be able to make her laugh within minutes of them meeting. They turn to me as I walk up to them.

"Samantha," Margaret says. "Dean and I were just discussing the details of our arrangement. Dean said he could get a couple performers, and we could start clown classes as soon as next week."

"That's great!" I exclaim. "The kids seemed to enjoy it."

"I'll be in touch with more details," Dean says. Margaret nods and walks away. I squeeze Dean's arm and grin at him.

"That's amazing! She loved it! She's never that enthusiastic!"

"That was enthusiasm?" he asks as he glances towards the woman. I laugh and nod. He swings his eyes back to me. "Where did you go just then? Margaret said someone wanted to meet you."

My face falls as I think of the woman in the hallway. I look up at Dean and can still see the gleam in his eyes from his performance, and I don't have the heart to dampen his spirits. Who cares if someone warned me off him! I know he comes from a rich family, and so far he's chosen me every time. Nothing has hinted that he would do anything different.

I shake my head. "Just a parent," I lie. "Come on, I should go home." I open my mouth, wanting to tell him about the baby but nothing comes out. What if the woman was right, and he'll freak out? What if he doesn't want to be with me at all?

He puts his arm around my shoulder and kisses the side of my head. "Oops!" he says as he licks his finger and wipes at my temple. "Forgot I had all this makeup on," he laughs.

I chuckle. "Do you need me to clean you up and undress you again?" I ask with an eyebrow raised, thinking of the very first day in the hospital parking lot.

"Need?" Dean grins. "I don't think I need you to, but the real question is do I want you to undress me." He wiggles his overdrawn clown eyebrows. "The answer is yes."

I laugh and tap his arm lightly. "You have to wash that off

first," I say. "I know you love being a clown but there's nothing sexy about it."

"Nothing?" he says in a sultry voice as he licks his lips and pretends to unbutton the fluffy red buttons down his front. I laugh again and nod to the door.

"Come on, you. Let's go."

He laughs and swings his arm around my shoulder, leaning over to plant a sloppy kiss on my cheek as I laugh and try to push him off. We gather his things and head out towards our cars to head back home. I give him a kiss after we finish loading everything in the car and search his eyes. I looks at me, questioning my stare. I just smile and kiss him again before we part ways for the night.

He wouldn't betray me, I know he wouldn't. He wouldn't choose money over me, would he? I touch my stomach and glance at him from my car. Everything seems a thousand times more complicated with this baby inside me.

34

DEAN

AFTER I SAY goodbye to Sam, I pack my equipment in my car and head home. I feel good. I had a great show with the kids, Sam's boss seemed to like me, and Pat will be happy to have a new partnership with the after school program. My new job is going well, and Sam and I are stupidly happy together.

I lug all my props and my costume over to the elevator and carry it up to my floor. I shuffle the big box from one hand to the other and find my keys. I'm focused on balancing everything in my hands and I swing the door open, holding it ajar with my foot as I shuffle inside. I drop the box onto the floor and let out a big sigh, stretching up tall and running my fingers through my hair.

My mother's voice makes me jump out of my skin. I stumble backwards and whip around to see her sitting at my kitchen table.

"Mom!" I exclaim.

"Dean," she says. She stands up and walks towards me slowly. I adjust my clothing, still wearing my clown suit tied around my waist. My mother's eyes drift down and she scoffs. She hands me a piece of paper.

"What's this?" I ask. Instead of answering, she nods to the paper and I unfold it slowly. I frown as my eyes scan the page. "What is it, a contract?"

"*Your* contract," she corrects. "Clause 42.B. The non-compete agreement." Her eyes narrow as she looks me up and down. "Last time we spoke I told you I'd give you three months to think it over with Victoria. And time is almost up."

"What does this have to do with anything?" I ask, waving the paper at her. She sighs and shakes her head.

"Well, it seems that the time for reflection didn't convince you to play by our rules. Looks like you've gotten yourself a new little girlfriend. So maybe this will change your mind. Read the clause."

I shiver as she mentions Sam and flick my eyes down to the page. I scan the paper again and I read the heavy legal writing. I frown. "This says I can't work for any investment firm for five years after I leave Dad's firm!"

"Ding ding ding!" she says with a bitter laugh. "It seems you've breached the terms of your contract by getting yourself a new job." She takes a step towards me and runs her finger down my cheek. "And as much as I'm proud of my boy for being so resourceful, I won't hesitate to make sure to punish you to the full extent of the law."

"Mom..." I say, frowning. "What am I supposed to do! I need a job. This is all I know how to do."

"You're supposed to dump that little whore you've found yourself and marry the fucking woman we chose for you."

"Don't call her that."

"Fine. The selfless children's program director from

fucking Virginia. Really, Dean? A girl from a small town in a dead-end job? You're giving up your future for *her*?"

"I'm not giving anything up," I shoot back. "I'm giving up the future that you and dad had planned out for me. For yourselves! When are you going to understand that I'm my own person. I'm not going to throw my life away in a fucking loveless marriage just because my parents told me to!"

My mother sighs and shakes her head. "I hoped it wouldn't come to this. If you don't come back to the family, not only will we sue you for breach of contract, but you'll never see Samantha again."

My heart drops to my stomach and my brow knits together. "What does that mean?" I ask slowly, not wanting to betray the panic that's rising in my throat.

My mother waves her hand and straightens her jacket. She pats her hair down in that familiar motion, making sure not a single hair is out of place.

"It means what it means," she finally says, swinging her eyes over to me. "Look at where we are, Dean. We're up on the tallest, thinnest branch of the tree. You don't get here without leaving some people behind."

"What does it fucking mean," I say, taking a step towards her. "Don't you fucking dare hurt her, or—"

"Or what," she interrupts. My chest is heaving up and down as I try to understand what she's saying. "You'll hurt us? You'll sue us? My dear son," she says, taking a step towards me. "You are nothing. You have nothing. You've been able to keep your bank accounts, your apartment, and your new job because I've allowed you to. But now, my patience is wearing thin."

She grabs her bag and steps around me, turning around when she gets to the door. "Break up with the girl today, and show up to your father's office tomorrow morning. There are no other options. Your time is up."

With that, she swings the door open and walks out. All the air in my lungs goes out with her and I slump down onto a chair. I'm breathing heavily, head in hand, trying to figure out what the fuck just happened.

She threatened me, she threatened Sam, she threatened to take everything away from me. As good as it felt to be independent, I don't doubt that she'd be able to close my accounts and lock me out of everything I have.

"Fuck!" I yell, slamming my palm down on the table. "Fuck fuck fuck!" Every word comes with another slam. I grab the contract she brought me and rip it into a thousand pieces, throwing them across the room. They flutter down, taunting me as they fall one by one at my feet.

I take a deep breath. I don't have to break up with Sam. I can figure this out.

As soon as the thought crosses my mind, I know it's not true. They're too powerful, they have too much control over me, and I know that they'll stop at nothing to make their dreams of political success come true. I'm not their son anymore, I'm an obstacle in the way of their rise to the top. It feels like a dagger in my heart. After everything I've done, all the hours I've put in at work, all the time I've spent trying to be a good son... it means nothing.

What can I do?

I can run away. I can tell Sam to pack a bag and I can drain my accounts and run away. I grab my phone, ready to call her and tell her before slumping back down in a chair.

She'll think I'm crazy. There's no way she would agree. And plus, where would we go? My parents have friends all over the country, all over the world! They'd find us, they'd hurt her, and they'd force me to marry Victoria.

No, I can't put Sam through that. My priority has to be to keep her safe. What's that thing that people say, when you love something you have to let it go? Maybe that's what this is.

I don't realize I'm crying until I feel the tears falling off my chin. I bring my hands up to my face and sob, my whole body shaking. It takes me a long time to accept that in order to protect Sam, I need to get her as far away from me as possible.

35

SAMANTHA

I PULL up in front of Jess's house and take a deep breath. I probably should have told him about the baby, but I just couldn't find the words. I'll tell him next time I see him. I think about his performance and smile.

The kids were so happy when Dean was performing, and they were already asking about juggling lessons. I think he'll be one of the more popular acts. Even if we could schedule Dean or one of the other entertainers for one night a month it would make a big difference to the program.

My mind is buzzing with all these thoughts as I grab my purse and head inside. The second I open the door, I hear one of the twins screaming. I walk down the hall and Jess appears, her hair sticking up in all directions as she rushes out of the twins' bedroom.

"Sam, hi!" she breathes. "Would you mind grabbing Matt's blankie? I think it's on the sofa. I have to grab Michelle."

"No problem," I say. I glance at her from the corner of my

eye, seeing how frazzled she is for the first time. She sighs as she moves some of my things off the coffee table and I cringe. For the first time since I got here, I feel like I'm in the way. And now, with the child inside me, I know I'll definitely be overstaying my welcome.

I grab Matt's blanket and bring it in to him, doing my best to quiet him down while Jess takes Michelle. Once the twins are quiet and finally asleep, I head to the kitchen and pour two cups of tea. Jess takes it gratefully. She shakes her head.

"It isn't getting any easier," she says.

"I know. Listen, I don't mean to be in the way here, so I was thinking I would start looking for a place of my own. With the baby..." I pause, glancing at Jess's reaction. Her face stays steady and she nods slowly.

"You're not in the way, Sam. I hope you don't feel like you have to leave. You're welcome to stay as long as you need to. Have you spoken to Dean?"

I shake my head. "Not yet."

"Maybe he'll want to move in together," she says.

I sigh. "I don't even know if he'll want the baby," I say.

"Why don't you stay here a little longer, Sam. Your life is going to be upside down soon."

I smile. "You guys have been so great and it's time I leave you to your family."

Jess nods and sighs. "I can help you go to viewings if you want." She takes a drink and sighs again. "I'm exhausted. I need to go to bed while the two of them are sleeping."

I nod. "I'll clean up," I say as she drops her mug in the sink. Soon I'm alone in my friend's kitchen, wondering how I'll find a place of my own. I can start looking online tonight and see what there is on the market. Maybe I could even move closer to work and closer to Dean, that way I wouldn't be spending so much time in the car. I brush my hand over my stomach and shake my head. Maybe I'm being ridiculous, and moving is just going to add extra stress.

A small flame of excitement builds as I think of having my own space and starting a family of my own. I need to tell him about the baby first, before I make any rash decisions.

I pull out my phone and find Dean's number.

Sam: I've been thinking I'll move out of Jess's. How do you feel about helping me view some shoebox apartments?

I smile as I press send and head towards my bedroom. Something catches my eye as I walk by—the brown box. I grab it off the shelf and turn it around in my hand. I take a deep breath. I finally feel like my own person, and I finally feel like I'm completely over Ronnie. I can deal with whatever's in this box. Once I'm in my bedroom, I rip the brown paper off the box and open it up. I frown as I look at the contents.

It's a red clown's nose with a scrap of paper. The scrap of paper has the same sharpie writing as the box, with four words scrawled across it.

GO BACK TO VIRGINIA.

My heart starts to beat harder and my mouth is suddenly dry. Go back to Virginia?? Is this a threat? The red clown nose obviously means Dean. This can't be from Ronnie, it was on the front steps the day he showed up here. He almost got in a fight with Dean, and they'd never met before. I turn the paper over and look in the box again. There's nothing else.

My thoughts turn back to the woman in the hallway.

Could she have sent it? She knew my name, and I had no idea who she was. What the fuck is going on?

My cell phone buzzes.

Dean: We need to talk.

My chest feels hollow and somehow my mouth gets even drier. I fucking know we need to talk, Dean. All of a sudden my hands are trembling and I try to think of something to answer. Should I tell him about this? I stand up and pace back and forth when the doorbell rings.

My heart is thumping as I glance down the hallway towards the front door. I walk slowly, each step creaking on the wooden floors as I make my way to the front. My heartbeat is roaring in my ears by the time I get to the door. I wish Jess had a peep hole and the panic starts to rise inside me.

I take a deep breath and shake my head. I'm being ridiculous. With a sudden gust of courage, I rip the front door open and stare outside. I take a step back in surprise when I see a woman on Jess's front steps. She's perfectly put together, standing with her hands clasped in front of her body. Her cold smile makes a shiver travel down my spine.

"Hello, Samantha," she croons. I try to swallow, licking my lips to get some moisture back in my mouth. How does she know my name? She looks familiar somehow, like I've seen her before. I frown.

"Who are you?" I croak back in response. Instead of answering, she hands me a large yellow envelope. I hesitate before taking it from her. I turn it around and then glance back at the woman. She nods to the envelope.

"Open it."

I glance from her to the envelope and unhook the string holding it closed. I open it up and pull out a stack of papers.

They look familiar, and it takes me a few seconds to realize these are my divorce papers.

"What the fuck?" I say, staring at her. "How did you get these? Who are you?"

She just smiles at me. "I want you to stop seeing my son."

The recognition finally clicks and I see a hint of Dean in her features. My jaw drops open and I shake my head.

"No! Why? What's going on? Why do you have these?"

"Unfortunately, it seems your lawyer never filed them," she says slowly. "And your ex doesn't seem too happy about your relationship. He might want to renegotiate some of the terms in a way that's… more palatable to him. A judge might not like the fact that you've jumped into bed with another man so soon after your separation. It might raise certain questions about your fidelity."

"My fucking fidelity?" I repeat, jaw hanging down. "Are you serious? *He's* the one who cheated on *me*! *He's* the one who broke *my* heart! How did you get these! I'm calling the police."

She shakes her head and smirks. "No you aren't. You're going to stop seeing my son, and those divorce papers will get filed. If they don't, you're in for a very long, very expensive legal battle where your name will be dragged through the mud. You'll never work with children again."

She flings the last words at me and they hit me as if they had physical weight. I stagger backwards and stare at her, trying to understand what's going on. She gives me that cold smile again and turns around, walking slowly down the steps as a driver steps out of her waiting car and opens the back door for her. She glances at me once more before sliding in. The driver closes the door and walks around to the driver's seat before speeding off down the road.

I stare after them until they're out of view and then swing the door shut. My eyes drop to the stack of papers in my hands and then back out to the street.

What is going on? Why doesn't she want me to date Dean? How did she get these papers? Where is Ronnie? Who is she, and more importantly, who the fuck is Dean?! Who have I been dating for the past two months??

36

DEAN

THE PHONE KEEPS RINGING and ringing and ringing. Sam isn't picking up. The last text I got from her was about moving out of Jess's place. I toss my phone aside, blowing all the air out of my lungs. I bring my hands up to my face and groan as I lean on my elbows.

What a mess.

I'm going to be honest with Sam. That's the best way. I'll be honest about Victoria, about being pressured to marry her, about my parents' political aspirations, everything. I'll tell her about my mother's threats and then she'll be able to make her own mind up.

My phone is still dark and silent, and I pick it up to dial her number one last time. I know I shouldn't. It's late, and she's probably asleep, but there's still a niggling thought that tells me something else is going on. She usually sends me a message before she goes to bed, and tonight I've heard nothing from her.

I replay everything my mother said and sigh again. She wanted me to break up with Sam tonight and report back to my father tomorrow. That gives me no time to figure anything out.

I can't take this anymore. I need to see her, I need to talk to her and tell her what's going on.

I grab my jacket and rush out the door. I'll drive to her place and make sure she's alright. From there, we'll be able to figure something out together. I jog to the elevator and tap my foot as it makes a slow ascent towards my floor. I sigh, counting the seconds until the doors ding open.

It seems to take an eternity to go back downstairs and I rush to my car. It seems like every single light is a red light and it takes me forever to get to her place.

Finally, I pull up outside and jump out. I ring the doorbell and shift my weight from foot to foot until I hear someone coming towards the door. I breathe a sigh of relief when Sam opens the door.

"What are you doing here?" she asks, brows knitting together on her forehead.

"I was worried about you, I had to see you," I reply.

"Why would you be worried?" Her words seem to have a double meaning and she stares at my face intently. A lump forms in my throat and I'm struggling to find the words to tell her what I need to tell her. Where do I start! Her eyes narrow a bit more and I shake my head.

"You weren't answering my calls," I finally concede. "I…"

She waits for me to go on and finally shakes her head. "What the fuck is going on, Dean? Why is your mother showing up on my doorstep and telling me to break up with you? Why some woman showing up at my work and telling me you aren't what you seem? Why are you suddenly worried about my welfare? What is going on?"

"Wait, what? She came here?! And who was at your work?"

"Tell me what's going on Dean, it feels like there are way too many secrets you're not telling me."

"There aren't any secrets! It's just family stuff."

She nods slowly. "Just family stuff. Right. The family that owns your life and basically runs this town. And you wouldn't want to share any of that with me, because I'm not part of your world, is that it? I'm just a fun distraction? It's not until your own mother, who I've never met before, comes to my door that you're suddenly worried about me knowing these things?"

"No, Sam! What? No! Not at all!"

"Leave me alone, Dean. I dealt with secrets and lies in my marriage and I'm sure as hell not going to deal with it from you."

"Wait, Sam, please," I say, taking a step towards her. Her face softens and she sighs.

"You need to be honest with me, Dean. I can't take this."

My heart breaks and I nod. "They're pressuring me to break up with you. I swear Sam, I'm trying to fight it. It's not you, they've wanted me to marry someone else. I just need a little time to figure it out."

She chews her lip and stares at my face. "I need to think, Dean. And you need to give me some answers."

"I will. I promise. I can't take you out tonight, I'm pretty sure my mother is watching me. Meet me tomorrow after work? I'll know more then."

She nods. We stand there in front of each other silently until Sam's face relaxes and she starts to smile. The squeezing in my chest disappears and I relax. I take a step forward and kiss her softly. The minute our lips touch, relief floods through me and I pull away.

"I'll pick you up from work and I'll tell you everything," I say. She nods. "Goodnight, Sam."

"Goodnight," she says. She sighs and shakes her head before slowly closing the door.

I get back in my car and let out a sigh. That wasn't what I was expecting. My mother must have come here right after going to my place. She must have threatened Sam somehow, and what was she saying about someone showing up at her work?

The panic that I felt earlier starts to transform into anger. I can feel it curling in my stomach as I think about my mother and father and Victoria. They've controlled my life for far too long. I don't know how I'm going to get out of this one, but I do know that Sam cares about me and she wants to be with me. I want to tell her everything and she wants to hear it, and that's got to count for something.

I'll go see my parents tomorrow morning and try to stall for time. That's all I need, more time. I need time to talk to Sam and time to figure out how I'm going to get out from under my parent's thumb. I need to figure out what they have over Sam and how to make sure they won't come after either of us.

I can figure it out, I know I can, but I need more time.

With a deep breath, I start the car. Before I can pull out, the passenger's door opens and a large man gets in. I turn around to protest when I see the man's face. I know that face.

"How have you been enjoying fucking my wife?" he says. My jaw drops as I realize who it is.

"Ronnie? What are you doing? Get out of my car!"

Something glints in his hand and I see the barrel of a gun.

My chest suddenly feels hollow and a lump forms in my throat. I flick my eyes back to his face and see him snarl.

"I had the honor of meeting your mother when I came here the first time. Apparently she likes to have you followed and she saw an opportunity. And what can I say, I'll take any opportunity to fuck your life up after you swooped in and took Sam from me."

"That psychotic bitch," I breathe, "and Sam was over you the moment you cheated on her, you bastard." He flicks the gun forwards and growls.

"Drive."

37

SAMANTHA

I WAKE up with a pounding headache. It feels like I'm hungover, even though I haven't had a single drink. I groan as I get out of bed. I get ready for work as if I'm on autopilot. I brush my teeth and wash my face, trying to ignore the sense of dread in my stomach.

I'm pregnant.

I still can't get over that. *I'm on the pill,* I just keep thinking over and over. My thoughts drift from the baby to Dean to his family. I splash water on my face and lean against the bathroom counter, droplets of water falling into the sink.

I let all the air out of my lungs and take a deep breath to stop myself from crying. I don't know if I can do this, but somehow I do. I get dressed and have coffee and make it to work on time. I talk to Margaret and the minutes tick by.

By the time the kids are coming in after school, I feel like a zombie. One of them latches onto my leg and a pain passes through my heart.

I don't want to do this alone.

I ruffle the kid's hair and try to blink back my tears. The little boy smiles at me and tugs at my hand.

"What's wrong, Mrs Samantha? You look sad."

"I'm not sad at all, Joey. I'm happy to see you today!"

"Is Clifford the clown here today? I want to learn how to make a balloon monkey!"

My heart squeezes and I force a smile. "He'll be back soon, kiddo. You can learn how to make all kinds of animals. Now go see Mrs. Margaret, we're going to start the game soon."

He smiles at me again and runs towards my boss. My shoulders relax as I watch him run away. His friends come join him and pretty soon the room is full of children. Their laughter is like a healing balm on my heart, and soon the tension in my body starts to ease. I stretch my neck from side to side and take a deep breath.

If I have to do this alone, I will. Right now, the most important thing is making sure this baby is safe. I check my phone once again and frown when I see it blank. Usually Dean would have contacted me by now, especially since we had plans to meet after work.

I slip my phone back into my pocket and square my shoulders. I'll listen to what he has to say, but I have to prepare myself for the possibility that it could be over between us. Even without the baby, something's going on with his family. Until I know what it is, this baby has to stay a secret. Until I know that the three of us are safe and free, I have to carry this secret around with me.

I brush my hand over my stomach and feel an overwhelming sense of love come over me. It's not a burden, this secret. It's a gift. I look around the room at the children laughing and playing and I feel scared and calm at the same time.

If my heart is about to be broken and I have to say goodbye to Dean, at least I'll have a part of him to carry around with me. I'll have a child to love and take care of, and I'll be able to be the best mother that I can possibly be.

It really is a gift.

My phone buzzes in my pocket and I rush to grab it. My heart sinks when it isn't Dean's name.

Jess: You okay?
Sam: Bit rough but okay. Starting to think I can do this.
Jess: You can. You're strong.

I read the four words over and over and over until I start to believe them. I can do this. I'm strong. I can take care of this baby, and I can face whatever it is that Dean has to tell me. Whatever it is, it won't destroy me. It can't, because now I have to be strong. I have to make it work for this baby.

It doesn't matter what Dean has to tell me, and as much as I want to ride off into the sunset with him, I don't need him. I read Jess's message again.

You can. You're strong.

With a deep breath, I head back towards the group of children. I stand a bit taller and smile a bit wider. I can do this. I'm strong.

38

DEAN

"Why are you keeping me here? Let me go!" I yell out through the shitty motel's old door. I hear Ronnie and the other man shuffle outside but the door doesn't open. For the thousandth time, my eyes swing around the room. There's no windows or doors except the front door and front window, and the two men are guarding it day and night.

I sigh, sitting back down on the bed. I haven't slept at all. They took my wallet, keys, phone, everything I had on me. I check the time and my heart squeezes. I wonder where Sam is. I wonder if she's safe. He must have been waiting outside her house, or maybe he was following me?

"You'll be arrested!" I call out again. "I'll get a restraining order! Stay away from Sam!" I yell. One of the men bangs on the door and I quiet down. I remember the way the barrel of his gun dug into my side when he pushed me in the door and I groan, letting my head drop into my hands.

I never thought I'd say this, but I actually would prefer to be with my mother and father right now than here in this motel. I glance at the clock and groan. I'm late for my meeting with my father, which means they'll be going after Sam. I get up and press my forehead to the door.

"I need my phone! Please! Just one phone call!"

"Shut the fuck up!" comes the response through the door. I sigh and turn around. I grab the pillows off the bed and throw them on the ground, yelling and stomping on them as I try to release some of the pressure that's building inside me.

I hear a noise at the door and I spin around, expecting to see Ronnie's lumbering body in the doorway. Instead, I frown as a different figure appears.

"Mom?!"

"Dean," she says. "May I come in?"

"Are you behind this?? Is this you?? What the fuck is going on!" My jaw drops as my eyes flick between her and Ronnie.

"I'll take that as a yes," she answers, stepping through the doorway. Her nose scrunches ever so slightly as her eyes swing around the room. I'm guessing she's never been anywhere like this in her life. The carpet has a big brown stain on it, the old brown floral wallpaper is peeling off the walls and the ceiling is covered in water stains. She stands inside and pulls the door closed.

"Now," she says. "Are you ready to come back to the family?"

"Hold the fuck up," I say, turning towards me. "Are you telling me that you fire me, you cut me off, you threaten me, threaten my girlfriend, and then you have me followed, you kidnap me, and you expect me to roll over and agree to marry someone who betrayed me? You expect me to ever speak to you again? What the fuck is wrong with you?"

My mother sighs and shakes her head. "You always were a

high spirited child, Dean. Your father didn't want to take these measures but I knew it would be the only way go get you to agree to our terms."

She drops an envelope on the bed beside me and nods to it. I pick it up slowly and pull out a stack of pictures. It's me and Victoria, sharing a coffee at one of the cafes near my apartment. I flick through the photos to see the two of us kissing and laughing.

"What the fuck is this?" I ask.

"Those are some pictures we had on file."

"On file?! You were having me followed?! These must be a year old or more, when that bitch and I were still together. You had someone take pictures of us?? What the actual fuck?!"

My mother waves a hand to dismiss my protests. "We only wanted to make sure you were protected. There were some threats to the family at the time and I didn't want you to worry."

My head is spinning. I try to make sense of what my mother is saying but none of it makes any sense. I take a deep breath and take a step towards her.

"You want me to believe that you had someone follow me and take photos of me for my own protection? What 'threats against the family'?" The anger inside me is reaching a peak as my mother sighs. She takes a step forward and puts a perfectly manicured hand on my forearm. When she looks into my eyes, I see nothing but harness in her eyes.

"Those pictures are on their way to Samantha. Victoria will hand-deliver them. I wanted to make sure you'd break up with her yesterday, but Ronnie here tells me you did just the opposite. It's over between the two of you."

My jaw drops. "You're going to lie to her and make her

believe I'm *cheating* on her?! That will destroy her. Mom! Stop. Call her!"

"No."

My mother squares her shoulders and looks up at me. Her lips curl into almost a snarl and she shakes her head. "It's over. You're marrying Victoria and you're working for your father."

Panic starts to rise inside me like a volcano. I glance around the room, through the window at the two men and back at the pictures in my hands. I shake my head.

"No," I whisper. "No, I can't."

"You have no choice. If you so much as go anywhere near Sam, we'll have to get rid of her."

"Get rid..? Mom, who are you? Who the fuck are you?"

"Grow up, Dean. You don't get rich being nice." She knocks on the door and it swings open. Ronnie's face appears and I growl at him.

"How the fuck did you get involved. What does she have over you? Ronnie, you don't need to do this!" My mother waves her hand and the two men approach me, guns pointing directly at my stomach. I throw my hands up and feel my bottom lip start to tremble. I hate how scared I am.

"Stop, please," I say. They grab me roughly on either side and drag me to a waiting car. I see my mother drive off ahead of us before I'm thrown in the back seat and driven away from that godforsaken motel.

My heart feels like it's been shattered. Sam will never speak to me again, and if I try to tell her the truth they'll kill her. I have to do what my mother wants. I have to marry Victoria. My chest tightens at the thought until it feels like I'm being squeezed to death. I watch the cars and buildings rush by out the window as we drive towards my father's office. Tears prickle my eyelids. .

The only way to keep Sam safe is to break her heart, and to break my own at the same time.

39

SAMANTHA

THE DAY HAS DRAGGED ON. I glance at the clock again as the kids start to file out. Dean still hasn't contacted me. As much as I force myself to believe that I can do it, the weight that dropped onto my shoulders at the doctor's office is still there. My heart beats a little bit faster when I think about telling Dean about the baby.

Should I tell him right away? I know I should wait until everything with his family blows over. But maybe it would change his mind? I jerk my head up when I hear my name.

"...Samantha?"

"Sorry, Margaret. I was in a world of my own there."

"Are you feeling okay? I was just going to say that you can head home if you want to. I've got everything under control here."

"Are you sure? It was supposed to be my night to set up for tomorrow."

She smiles kindly and nods her head. "Go home, Samantha. I'll see you tomorrow. And tell Dean to call me! I was expecting to hear from him or his boss today, we have a lot to organize with the children's clown school days."

"He's been busy today," I say, not wanting to tell her that I haven't heard from him either. "I'm supposed to go see him now so I'll make sure to tell him."

"Thank you. Have a good night."

I head out the door and shuffle to my car. I sit down and let out a sigh, turning the car on to let the air conditioning blow onto my face. I close my eyes for a few moments, letting my hand drift to my stomach.

How did this happen?

I mean, I know how this happened. But *how did this happen*?!

Dean's mother's face appears in my mind and I shudder. She was ready to ruin my life if I kept speaking to Dean, threatening to drag my name through the mud. And now with a baby on the way I can't imagine what she'd threaten me with.

The thought of her using this baby against me makes my blood run cold. I sit up a bit straighter and open my eyes, gripping the steering wheel as I sit in the parking lot.

The realization dawns on me then—the realization that I can't tell Dean. I can't tell him about the baby until I know what's going on with his family. I can't risk her finding out and putting me or the baby in danger. I can't risk it. I let my hand fall to my stomach again and take a long breath.

First, I need to figure out what's going on. I need to find Dean and demand an explanation. Once I know that, I can figure out whether or not I can tell him about this baby. If I have to do it alone to protect it, then so be it.

With renewed energy, I turn the key in the ignition and the car rumbles to life. I send Dean a quick message to tell him to meet me at Jess's. For the first time today I feel alive. I feel like I can face this, and I can figure it out. I'm not alone anymore, I'm not waiting for Dean to explain anything. I'm sure as hell not going to let Dean's mother push me or my baby around. I flick on the radio and head home, singing alone to every song that I know.

By the time I pull up to Jess's house, I feel like at least part of the weight on my shoulders has been lifted. I check my phone before going in and purse my lips when I see it's still blank.

"Come on, Dean," I say to myself. It's more important than ever for me to see him and figure out what the heck is going on.

I jog up the steps when something catches my eye. It's a brown envelope sticking out from under the welcome mat. It's exactly like the one Dean's mother had with my divorce papers in it, . I lean down and pick it up, glancing up and down the street. There's no one there, or at least no one who looks like they delivered the envelope. I flip it over but it's blank, so I open up the top.

My heart sinks like a stone when I pull out the photos. I flick through them one by one, seeing Dean with a woman. I frown and squint as I look at the pictures more closely as my chest gets that horrible hollow feeling and my head starts to feel light. I know that woman! She's the one who came to my work, the one who told me Dean wasn't all he appeared to be.

My heart starts hammering against my ribcage and I flick through the photos again. I shake my head as I see images of Dean and the woman, laughing and kissing and smiling and all I can do is whisper *no, no, no*. I stuff the photos back inside the envelope and rush in the door. I barely glance at Jess as I hurry to my bedroom, closing the door behind me and falling down onto my bed.

The tears start stinging my eyes and I brush them away angrily.

Was she telling the truth? Was she trying to tell me that I shouldn't trust him because he was cheating on me with her?

There's that word—*cheating*. Even thinking it leaves a bitter taste in my mouth. I thought I'd never feel this again, not after Ronnie. I thought I was done with it. I open the envelope and look at the photos again, more slowly this time. My vision starts to blur as the tears start streaming down my face and I shake my head.

"It can't be true," I whisper to myself. "It just can't be true."

My hands are trembling and my eyes are so full of tears that I can't see anything anymore. I let them fall down my cheeks and I cover my face with my hands. His betrayal pierces me like a hot dagger through the heart. I sit on the edge of my bed and cry, my mouth open in a silent sob as I try to hide my pain from the rest of the house. I shake and shudder and wrap my arms around my stomach as my whole body crumples over. I rock back and forth and let the tears fall down my face.

I only realize I wasn't being quiet at all when Jess appears by my side. Her arms are around me and she's holding me against her chest, stroking my hair and cooing. I feel her reach over towards the photos and look at them before wrapping her arms around me a little bit tighter.

I want to tell her about Dean's mother, and about the other woman, and Dean showing up last night. I want to tell her everything but she's been so stressed and tired these days that it just seems selfish to burden her more. And now…

"Come on, Sam. There, there. Come on," she coos. I sniffle and choke and sob until I feel empty again.

Finally, I'm able to look up at her. She shakes her head.

"What happened?"

"I don't know! Dean's mom threatened me and that woman warned me and now Dean is worried and he won't talk to me and I'm pregnant and it's all a bit mess and I should have just stayed in Lexington." I run out of breath and stop talking as I inhale. Jess's face is a picture of complete confusion.

"Wait, what?"

I sob again and try to wipe my eyes. "I don't know what to do, Jess."

"Tell me what happened. Who gave you these pictures?"

I finally wipe the tears away and am able to see her a little bit more clearly. I take a deep breath and start talking.

40

DEAN

When I walk into my father's office it's like nothing has happened. Everyone says hello to me as if I've been working there for the past two months. I'm led to the big corner office and I slump down in a chair with my head in my hand. My mother and father are looking at me expectantly. All I can do is nod. My mother claps her hands in front of her face.

"Good! That's settled."

She smiles at me and a shiver runs down my spine. My father's face is impassable, so I just stare at the carpet in front of me.

With that nod, I've agreed to their terms. I feel empty. I feel numb. I've just agreed to break up with Sam and to marry Victoria.

It's the only way to keep Sam safe. If I don't do what they say, they'll kidnap her exactly like me, except they won't let her go. My heart sinks even more and I take a deep breath. I have to do this.

I keep telling myself that I have to do this over and over.

Even so, I still shudder when I hear the clack-clack-clack of heels in the hallway and I see Victoria's face turn the corner into the office. There's a hint of panic inside me and I take a deep breath to calm myself.

I don't know if I can do this.

I close my eyes for a moment and think of Sam. I see her smile and the way she was with the kids at the organization. I see of the way she hops up excitedly when she's really happy about something. I map her body in my mind, remembering every freckle, every curve, every bone and muscle in her body. I'm anchoring all those memories in my mind. I might never see her again.

When I open my eyes again, all three of them are staring at me. I turn to Victoria and shake my head.

"I get why they're doing this," I say, pointing to my parents. "They've been wanting to go into politics since before I was born. But you?? What have you got to gain? Why are you doing this?"

She takes a step towards me and reaches her hand towards my face. I flinch away, not letting her fingertips touch my cheek. She grins.

"Poor, sweet, innocent Dean. You have no idea how rich you are, do you?"

"Is that what this is about? Money?"

"What else would it be about?" she snarls. "You think I'd actually want to be with you? Come on, Dean, grow up. You dress up like a fucking clown on the weekends."

The words sting. I've always known that none of them understand why I do the children's parties. I've always known that none of them have a generous bone in their bodies. But to have it thrown in my face like it's something to be ashamed of?

Sam's face appears in my head again. I see how happy she was when her boss agreed to let me give clown classes at the organization.

She gets it.

Not only does she get it, she lives it. Her whole life is dedicated to doing what I do for a couple hours a week: helping kids. She lives to give them just a bit of joy in any way she can.

"Right, so, the lawyer is almost done with the papers," my mother says, taking a step towards us. "We'll go to the courthouse tomorrow."

"Tomorrow!" I exclaim, turning to my mother. She sighs and rolls her eyes at me.

"Did you think you'd have time to change your mind? Yes, tomorrow. You will be married and you will do as we say, or else that sweet girlfriend of yours will pay the price."

I stare at my mother and feel something I've never felt before. I think it's hatred. I look at her perfectly manicured nails, her made-up face and her impeccable hair and all I see is fakeness. All I see is lies.

Hatred feels different than anger. It's stronger and more calm at the same time. My mother snarls and then relaxes. The heat of my hatred crawls down my spine and resting in the pit of my stomach. I can feel the blood pumping through my veins as my eyes swing from my mother to my father to my fiancee.

All three of them are completely relaxed, completely confident in their total victory over me. The blood pumps through my veins and my hatred curls from my stomach and expands in my chest. My father reclines in his chair and takes a deep breath that feels like a slap in the face. Victoria leans on the desk and my mother pats her hair down for the thousandth time.

I could scream. I could flip the whole desk over and smash this chair through the window. I could knock every book off the bookshelf and trash this entire office. I could go berserk and not calm down till the police came and tasered me.

I could, but I don't.

I think of Sam, and I know I can't. I think of Sam, and I know I have to stay here, sitting quietly, learning what true hatred feels like. I think of Sam, and I know that if I let go of her in my heart then that hatred will consume me.

I close my eyes and they start to fill with tears. I hear Sam's voice and hear her laugh. I can just about smell that perfume that I came to love. I hang onto every detail that I can remember, hang onto it before I'm overcome by my own hatred.

A deep, raking breath brings me back to the present. My father is saying something, and Victoria is looking at some papers of some sort. I should be listening, but it doesn't matter. I'll sign whatever they tell me to sign, I'll do whatever they tell me to do as long as I know they won't hurt Sam.

They have me where they want me, and there's nothing I can do about it.

All three of them turn to the door and stand up when it opens. I don't have the energy. I don't care who's there or what they have to say. It doesn't matter.

It's not until I take a deep breath that I smell the faintest hint of that floral perfume. My eyebrows draw together ever so slightly and something wakes up inside me. And then, like a breath of fresh air, she speaks.

"Hi, Dean."

I turn around slowly and see her silhouetted in the doorway. She looks as fierce as a lion, standing tall as she faces my parents and Victoria. My voice is just a croak as I say the name that's been on my lips for the past two months.

"Sam."

41

SAMANTHA

I can't even look at Dean. I know if I look at him, my courage might falter and I won't be able to do what I came here to do. I glance from Dean's mother to her father to the woman, Victoria. I know her name now. My whole body is trembling but I keep my gaze steady and my lips in a tight, thin line.

"Mr. Shelby, Mrs Shelby, Victoria," I say slowly. "I was hoping to find at least one of you here."

"What do you want?" Mrs Shelby barks. "I told you to mind your business. Don't you know Dean doesn't want you anymore? He had his fun and now it's over. Tell her, Dean!"

I force myself not to look at Dean. I keep my eyes steady on Victoria. Dean clears his throat.

"She's.. She's right, Sam. It's over."

The words pierce my heart and the pain radiates through my chest but I still don't look at him. It can't be true. I hang on to Jess's words and I squeeze my hands into fists. I keep my eyes on Victoria and pull out the envelope of pictures.

"Is this supposed to convince me?"

Dean makes a noise but I ignore him. Mrs. Shelby starts cackling.

"Don't be so desperate, girl. You heard him. It's over."

"It's only over because you said it was over," I say, swinging my eyes over to her. She takes a step backwards as if the force of my gaze is too much and I stand up ever so slightly taller. The tension in the air is thick and the room is completely silent except for my long, measured breaths. "Isn't it?"

Dean's mother spreads her stance and crosses her arms. She lifts her chin towards me and curls her lip into a snarl.

"So you're not as stupid as I thought you were," she barks. She cackles again and shakes her head, taking a step towards me. I stand my ground. "You don't belong in this world. Dean had his fun but now it's time for him to do his duty. Leave, and never come back, or else you know the consequences."

I try not to shiver at her words and take another breath.

"I'll leave, and I'll never come back. I'll never speak to Dean again," I say, trying to make my voice ring true. "I just want to hear it from you. Tell me he's with Victoria because you told him to be."

This time Victoria speaks. She spits her words at me with such venom it takes all my strength not to take a step back.

"That's right. He's here because he belongs here. With our two families joined, nothing will be able to stop us. He's a weak, pathetic man and if his parents weren't so rich I wouldn't even let him take my order at a restaurant. But I'll marry him and my family will carry his father's political career straight to the top. And I'll fuck whoever I want to fuck and crush his little heart over and over just because I can. So *leave*."

I try not to flinch at her words. I take a deep breath, swinging my eyes back to his mother.

"Thank you," I say slowly. "It's nice to hear the truth."

His mother laughs again. "The truth! The only truth is that our two families will run this city before the end of the year. Now get out."

My whole body is shaking and I spin on my heels. I hurry out of the office, rushing to the elevators and mashing the buttons to go downstairs. Once they open in the lobby, Jess rushes towards me.

"Did you get it?" she asks, breathlessly. "Are you okay?"

"I knew it," I say. "I fucking knew it. I knew those pictures had to be fake."

I pull out my phone and replay the recording I took. Just like we tested earlier, their voices are clear and you can hear every word that was said in that room. We look at each other and grin. My heart is pounding against my chest and I play the recording again.

"There it is," I breathe. "They admit it all. Threatening me, forcing him to get married, plotting to work together for politics. It's all there."

"Come on," Jess says. "Let's bury the bastards. Let's go to the police."

I close my eyes and take a deep breath. I can still see Dean out of the corner of my eye, head in hand as he sits slumped in that chair. He looked completely defeated, and his voice was dead when he told me he didn't want to see me. They have something over him, he was terrified. What would happen if I went to the police?

I shake my head. "We can't. What would they charge them with? Harassment? They haven't done anything wrong, not yet anyways. Nothing that we can prove. They have an army of lawyers and probably the police on their payroll. She got my divorce papers somehow, and she scared Dean into saying he didn't care about me. I don't know who they are, but they scare me. No, we can't go to the police."

"So what do you want to do? Sam, are you sure this is worth it? Maybe you should just let it go. Don't tell him about the baby, do it on your own. I'll help. Don't put yourself in danger for this guy!"

Jess's face is full of concern. She puts a hand to her cheek and shakes her head. I know what she's saying, and I get it. I just don't agree. I can't let Dean go, I can't turn my back on him and forget everything that's gone on between us. I've never met a man so genuine, a man who cares about me so much and who shares the same passions as I do. I've never met someone who can be a billionaire and a children's party clown on the same day. I've never met anyone who can make me laugh as easily or make me feel as good about myself.

I've never loved anyone like I love him. I can't let him go. I won't.

I look at the phone in my hand and take a deep breath. I know what I need to do. I need to beat them at their own game.

"What do you want to do, Sam?" Jess repeats.

I grin and pull out a business card I grabbed on the way out.

"Blackmail."

42

DEAN

My heart is broken. Shattered. There's a million shards of it floating inside me sending searing pain through my whole body.

Sam walked out the door and now I'm finished. I'm done. It's over. My life is completely over. She heard the truth, and she accepted it. I glance from my father to my mother to Victoria and I feel nothing but disgust. Disgust and hatred.

My father lifts his eyes to me and I see nothing in them. No regret, no love, no care. Nothing but coldness.

"You three are sociopaths," I finally say, shaking my head and leaning back in my chair. "You're complete sociopaths. Or psychopaths. I don't know the difference. You're fucked up."

"Oh shut up, Dean," Victoria says as she rolls her eyes. She flicks her hair behind her shoulder and raises an eyebrow towards me. "It's over."

"I know it's over, but that doesn't change the fact that you're all fucking psychopaths."

"Where were we?" My mother asks a bit too loudly.

"Henry, let's see the draft prenup agreement. Victoria, you've had a chance to review this?"

Victoria nods and my mother hands me the papers. I start scanning them and let out a gargled noise at the second page.

"A baby clause?! You want her to carry my child? You expect me to have sex with this fucking monster?" I say, waving the papers towards Victoria. "I agreed to marry her, I didn't agree to sleep with her!"

"You'll do what it says, Dean," my father growls. My eyes flick back to him and I shake my head.

"I can't. I can't fuck her. I can't even fucking look at her without dry heaving!"

"You never had a problem fucking me before," Victoria snarls.

"Yeah well that was before you cheated on me, you conniving bitch."

The vitriol in my voice surprises me. It's not like me to talk like this, or to feel like this. I've never had such hatred inside me. I thought my heart was broken when I found Victoria in my bed, but I was wrong. It's broken now. This is what it feels like. It's not just my heart that's broken, it's my whole soul, my whole being. The void that's been left behind is quickly filling with nothing but anger and bitterness. That sour loathing is starting to poison everything inside me.

Maybe I should just embrace it. If I'm going to be living in their world, I should become one of them. How else will I survive?

I don't even know what's happening. I sign some papers—the prenup, maybe. I'm in a daze. I'm led back outside and I get in the same car. Ronnie and his accomplice are still sitting in the front seat. We drive, and soon I'm back at the motel where they had me this morning.

No words are spoken between us as they drag me up to the same room. I get in and sit on the edge of the bed. I stare at the brown stain on the floor and take a deep breath.

This is it. This is my life now.

Sam's face appears in my head and I shake it away. I can't think of her, it'll only make me feel worse. I should just forget about her. It's for the best.

I sit on the edge of the bed until a the door opens. I look up, surprised to see the street lights on. I must have been sitting here for hours. Ronnie steps in with a styrofoam box. I smell food as he lifts the box up towards me.

"Dinner," he says. I grunt in response. He drops it on the little round table by the door and turns to leave.

"Wait!" I call out. He pauses and turns towards me. We stare at each other for a few moments until my face twists and I feel like my heart is breaking all over again.

"Why, Ronnie?" I finally croak. His eyes narrow and his lips press into a thin line. He stares at me for a long time and then glances out the door before closing it.

"What do you mean?" he answers.

"I mean why are you doing this? Why are you working for my mother? Don't you see that you're hurting Sam?"

Ronnie's face falls and he shakes his head.

"I didn't think it would go this far. She said she could get me a better settlement in the divorce if I helped her. And I saw you with her and you were making her laugh. You know how she looks when she laughs?" he looks at me and his face contorts. "I never thought that..." his voice trails off and he stares at the brown stain on the ground that I've been looking at for hours. He sighs.

"She's a monster," I finally say. "My mother. She's a monster. You should get as far away as possible."

Ronnie looks back up at me and all I see is pain in his face.

"I made a mistake. I lost everything. I couldn't…" his voice trails off and he looks through me. I watch his face harden. He stands up a bit taller and turns towards the door.

"Wait, Ronnie!" I call out. "Wait!"

The door slams.

"Fuck!" I exclaim. He doesn't want to be doing this. He thinks he has to, maybe he's in too deep. Maybe my mother knows too much about his past and his divorce. I shake my head. I thought we were understanding each other, I thought maybe he'd let me go. Maybe he'd let me call Sam.

I stare at the styrofoam box of food and finally get up off the bed. I flick it open to see a chicken drumstick and a pile of rice. I sigh, pushing the rice around with a plastic fork. I don't feel like a billionaire right now. I leave the food and fall down onto the bed. My eyes trace the outline of the water stains on the ceiling over and over until my eyelids get heavy and I fall asleep.

43

SAMANTHA

"Samantha Jane," Jess says with her hands on her hips. "You cannot blackmail the Shelbys. That's insane! You'll get yourself killed."

I look at my best friend and shake my head. "I have to," I say. "It's the only way to get Dean out of this."

"Fuck Dean!" she exclaims. "Seriously! Think of yourself! Think of the baby! You need to get away from these people. *Run.*"

Heads start to turn, so she grabs my arm and drags me out of the lobby. We head towards her car. I get into the passenger's seat, clutching my phone against my chest and then playing the recording again.

"Honestly, Jess, this would ruin a political career. Imagine the headlines: Billionaire Family Threaten Non-Profit Children's Worker," I say, fanning my arm out in front of me. Jess slams her door and shakes her head.

"Imagine this headline: Body of Deceased Non-Profit Worker Found in the Hudson River."

She raises an eyebrow and starts the car. I nod. She has a

point. They're obviously dangerous, and they've had these plans for a while. I have no idea what I'm up against. All I have is one measly recording. We start driving and pass a car in the parking lot.

"Jess! Is that Ronnie!?" I exclaim, craning my neck to see into the car. Jess slows to a stop and looks over. There are two men in the front of the car. They're talking to each other and looking towards the building. Jess looks at me, her face drawn with worry.

"What is he doing here?"

"Pull over up here. Let's see what they do," I say, pointing to a side road just ahead. Jess nods and turns the car around so we have a view of the front of the building. We say nothing to each other as we watch the other car. Jess sighs.

"This doesn't feel good, Sam. This feels very very bad."

I nod. There's a lump in my throat. She's right, it feels very bad. I look down at my phone and take a deep breath. Maybe she's right. Maybe this is too dangerous, and I should just run.

"How do you know Dean even wants to be saved? Didn't you say that he told you it was over? And those pictures..."

"They're not real! They admitted it up there. They told me that they were just using him."

"How do you know that! Who knows what's a lie and what's real."

I shake my head. "Dean doesn't want this. I know it, Jess. He wants to be with me."

"Sam," Jess starts. I hold up my hand and point to the front of the building.

"It's Dean," I breathe. He's being led to the car, and is thrown in the back seat. They drive towards us and we hide our faces as they drive by. I tap on the dash. "Come on, Jess. Let's see where they go."

She takes a deep breath but says nothing. We follow the black car from a short distance. Jess turns off the radio and we drive in complete silence. We follow them for just over half an hour until they pull up into a motel parking lot. I see Ronnie get out of the car and grab Dean by the arm. They push him up the stairs and throw him in a room. Ronnie and the other man sit down outside the room, guarding the entrance.

I turn to Jess. "We have to get him out. He's being held hostage!"

"Samantha. You have a baby on the way. Your ex husband is holding your new boyfriend in a shitty motel. His billionaire family threatened your divorce settlement and said they'd ruin your career. What do you want us to do? Go up there and ask Ronnie to let him out? Let's get the fuck out of here!"

The frustration builds inside me and I shake my head. Tears start prickling my eyelids and I look at Jess, pleading her with my eyes to understand where I'm coming from. She sighs and opens her arms up to give me a hug.

"Look, let's just go home for now. We can come back tomorrow morning and see what happens. Just sleep on it, please."

I nod. "Okay. Let's go."

Jess puts the car in gear and pats my leg. "It'll be okay," she says. "I promise."

I nod and turn my head, staring at the door where Dean disappeared until it's out of view.

By the time we get to Jess's place, my head is a mess. I don't know what to do. If I try to help Dean, I put myself and the baby in danger. If I don't help Dean, I'm abandoning him to his family. I collapse into bed and stare at the ceiling. I run my hands over my stomach and let the tears flow out of me.

I don't know what to do.

I hear Jess and her family making dinner and getting ready for bed. I don't have the energy to get up. I don't want to see her and Owen and the twins and be reminded of what a mess my life has become. All I want to do is lie here and forget about it all.

My phone buzzes and I frown.

Ronnie: I'm sorry. I never meant to hurt you.

My heart squeezes in my chest and the tears start to flow freely. I read the words over and over and all I feel is hurt and anger and betrayal all over again. I pick up the phone and dial his number. His voice is timid when he picks up.

"Sam?"

"What the fuck are you doing with him at that motel?" I growl into the phone. I hear Ronnie shuffle as if he's getting up and walking away.

"How do you know where I am?" he says in a hoarse whisper.

"Answer my question," I spit back. "Why are you texting me apologizing when you're keeping my boyfriend hostage. She got the divorce papers from you, didn't she?!"

"I'm sorry, Sam. I'm sorry," his voice breaks and I hear a sob. "I'm sorry. I'm sorry, Sam." He repeats it over and over and I try to stop him.

"Ronnie, get out of there! Go back to Lexington. What are you doing!"

He sobs once more and finally stops. "I can't," he says, his voice more firm. "I can't. Not until they're married. Then she'll let me go."

"When's that?" I ask, trying not to sound too forceful.

"I gotta go, Sam. I shouldn't be talking to you."

The phone clicks and I exhale. "Fuck!" I say under my breath. Dean's mother must be using the divorce over him as well. I lay back and stare at the ceiling. The fire in my stomach starts to burn hotter and my resolve strengthens.

Jess is right about a lot of things. She's right that this is dangerous and stupid and it might be suicide. But she's wrong about Dean. He's being held against his will and forced to marry someone who betrayed him. I sit up in bed and listen to the recording of our conversation again. I pull up Ronnie's name again and type a message.

Sam: *What does Mrs. Shelby have on you? Why is she making you do this?*

I grip my phone and hope he answers. If he does, I'll have two small but powerful bits of ammunition against them. If the recording doesn't scare them, maybe evidence of coercion and extortion will.

Ronnie: *She'll make me lose everything in the divorce. Her lawyers told me they'd leave me with nothing.*

I take a deep breath as I read the text over and over. Another one comes through.

Ronnie: *Wedding is tomorrow at the courthouse at 9am.*

I hold the phone to my chest and whisper a silent thank you. Ronnie may have betrayed me over and over, but for telling me this I'll forgive him everything. It doesn't matter, because now I can make everything right.

44

DEAN

I feel like I'm going to my own funeral. I've slept a couple hours, but when I see myself in the bathroom mirror it looks like I haven't slept in days. I sigh and splash some water on my face.

What's the point. It doesn't matter what I look like or how I feel, this wedding is going to happen anyways. I lean my hands against the mirror and close my eyes.

Sam.

I picture her laugh and the way her green eyes sparkle in the sun. I think of everything that I've anchored in my mind and I hang onto it. I'm doing this for her. I'm doing this to keep her safe.

I open my eyes and look at myself in the mirror before standing up a bit taller. I'm doing this for her. I can endure it all: the wedding, Victoria, my mother, my father. I can endure it all if I know that Sam is safe. I wipe my face clean and wait for Ronnie and the other man to lead me to the courthouse. I sit on the edge of the bed and stare at the stain on the carpet before lifting my eyes to the window.

I can do this. I can do this for her.

The drive to the courthouse feels short, too short. All too soon, Ronnie is opening my door and grabbing my arm to drag me out of the car.

"Alright, alright," I say, ripping my arm away. "I'm getting out. Let go of me."

He grunts and takes a step back. A gleaming black Rolls Royce pulls up behind us and my mother gets out, followed by my father, Victoria, and Victoria's parents. All five of them are dressed impeccably. I look down at my disheveled clothing and sigh.

Victoria takes a step towards me and I snort.

"Funny, I wasn't expecting you to wear white today," I snarl.

She rolls her eyes. "This wasn't the wedding I was expecting either, Dean. Get over it." She crinkles her nose and looks me up and down. "Would it have killed you to shower?"

"I'd rather you be disgusted with me," I retort.

Victoria opens her mouth to respond when my father makes a noise. He frowns as he looks at his phone screen.

"What is it, Henry?" my mother asks. My father lifts his eyes and frowns, his thick eyebrows drawing together like two grey caterpillars.

"That girl. She sent me this."

He turns the volume up on his phone and our voices ring out. My mother takes a step closer to his phone and her face freezes. The entire conversation when Sam was in the room is played over the speakers. I look at my mother, whose face starts to fall. It twists and contorts until she looks at Victoria and explodes.

"You just couldn't keep your fucking mouth shut, could you!"

Victoria flinches. Her face is completely pale and she shakes her head.

"It's okay. Daddy has the police commissioner in his pocket. She has nothing. She can't do anything with this. Right, Daddy?"

Victoria's father is beet-red. He looks like he's about to explode. All five of them look at each other and then at me.

"She'll go nowhere with this," my mother says.

"That's where you're wrong," Sam says. We all around to see her walking down the courthouse steps. She looks like an avenging angel, a halo of light around her as she walks towards us. She's standing tall, her hair falling in loose waves around her head. A light breeze lifts her hair and makes it flow behind her. Her chin is held high and her eyes are blazing as she stares at my mother.

"I have copies of that recording in more places than I can count. If anything happens to me or Dean, it's going straight to the press." She smiles gently and opens her palms towards us. "Political careers are made and broken in the press. Even a small town girl like me knows that."

My mother makes a gargled noise and takes a step towards Sam. Sam holds up a hand.

"If that doesn't work, I have evidence that you coerced Ronnie into threatening Dean."

With a gargled scream, my mother lunges towards Sam. Finally, the strength returns to my body and I jump between the two of them, holding my mother back before she can touch Sam.

My mother stops and lifts her eyes up to me. She looks at me with pure venom and I take a deep breath. I can feel Sam behind me and the fire of my family's hatred in front of me.

Slowly, I turn towards Sam who finally looks at me. My knees feel weak as her eyes break through the fire and anger inside me. Her presence is like a cold drink of water on a hot day, soothing the cracks on my heart and dulling the hatred inside me. I take a step towards her. I take a step towards love, towards goodness, towards Sam.

I can hear my father's protests but I ignore them. Sam extends a hand to me and I slip her fingers into my palm. The instant my skin touches hers I feel revitalized. I stand a little taller, my start to shoulders relax, and the tension in my face starts to fade. A small smile starts forming on her lips and she nods to me.

The two of us walk down the rest of the steps hand in hand and head off down the street. In this moment, I know that I'll never let her go. No matter who comes between us, what threats are leveled against me or her, I'm not going to let anyone hurt her or keep her away from me.

She's mine, and I'm hers. Nothing can keep us apart.

She squeezes my hand and guides me down the road. Once we round the first corner, she lets out a long breath and starts chuckling. Her laughter gets louder and her shoulders start to shake. After a few moments, the last bit of tension in my body disappears and we lean against each other as we laugh and laugh and laugh.

We walk a bit further until Jess rushes towards us. A torrent of emotions passes over her face when she sees us, from concern to confusion to finally a relieved smile.

"It's over," Sam says. "It's over. I was shitting my pants, but it's over."

Jess's face breaks open into a smile and tears start forming in her eyes. "Well what are you guys waiting for, kiss each other or hug or something! Don't just stand there laughing!" she says, laughing as she says it.

I turn to Sam and let my laughter fade, not needing any more encouragement to tilt her chin towards me and wrap her in my arms. I kiss her like I've never kissed anyone before. I kiss her with the knowledge that I'll never kiss anyone else, that she's the one for me and I'm the one for her.

45

SAMANTHA

I'M FLOATING, or dreaming, or dead and gone to heaven. I've never felt this good. Dean opens the door to his apartment and we glide in. He lets out a big sigh and my hand flutters to my stomach. I open my mouth to tell him about the baby but the words don't come. He looks at me and grins.

"What?" he says. "Why are you looking at me like that?"

I shake my head. "Nothing," I say. I don't know why I don't tell him about the baby. I don't want to ruin this moment. I don't want to change anything about his mood or the air between us. Right now, I just want to be with him and feel his arms wrapped around me and his lips on mine. Nothing more, and nothing less.

As if he reads my mind, he takes a step towards me and slides his hands over my waist. He pulls me into him and my arms wrap themselves around his neck. He rubs his nose back and forth over mine and lays a soft kiss on my lips before leaning his forehead against mine.

"I love you, Samantha. You're the strongest and most

courageous person I've ever met in my life. I can't believe you did that for me."

"For us," I correct. For us and our baby. My heart feels so full I think it might explode. He pulls me closer and I close my eyes to enjoy the heat of his body so close to mine. We stand there swaying gently from side to side until I open my eyes again and smile at him.

"I love you too," I whisper. His face breaks into a smile and he drops his hands to my bottom. He hoists me up and I wrap my legs around his waist.

We don't say anything, because there isn't anything to be said. He crushes his lips against mine as he carries me towards the bedroom. He lays me down onto the bed and presses his weight on top of me. I tangle my fingers into his hair and pull his kiss into me. My legs are still wrapped around his waist like I'm afraid to let go.

He runs his hand up my shirt and I shiver as his fingers leave a trail of sparks on my skin. The space between my legs is a ball of electricity, and I can feel his shaft pulsing against me.

We tear at each other's clothes, at each other's bodies. I kiss anything I come in contact with. I touch everything that my hands can reach, gripping and scratching and squeezing every part of his body. He groans as he devours me, covering my entire body with kisses. He moves to my hip and lays a kiss on it before looking up at me.

"I love this mole on your hip," he tells me.

I laugh. "Why?"

He shrugs and laughs with me. "I don't know. When I was sitting in that motel thinking my life was over, I was imagining you and all I wanted to do was kiss this mole."

"You're a weirdo," I laugh, running my fingers through his

hair. I smile and he dips his head back towards my hip, kissing my mole one more time.

The frantic energy between us slows down and our touch becomes tender. It's like we're learning each other's bodies for the first time all over again, running our hands over each other's bodies and trailing kisses behind them. His lips taste sweeter than I remember, and his body feels stronger and smoother than before.

When he enters me, I feel complete. He fills me up until my back arches and my lips fall open. He dips his head and bites my bottom lip as he pushes himself into me. Pain and pleasure mix as I cry out and let myself be carried away by bliss.

Our bodies dissolve into each other and we become one. We move together, moan together, kiss together, touch together, until I don't know where he ends and I begin. Our hearts beat as one.

When he comes, I come, and when I come, he comes. Our climax is like I've never felt before. Both bodies contract and arch and moan together and I feel his orgasm as viscerally as I feel my own. He's mine, and I'm his.

It's not until our heartbeats return to normal and my head is resting on his chest and I take a deep breath and feel like myself again. I run my fingers over and back across his chest as he strokes my hair.

"I love you," I whisper. My heart is beating in my chest and I feel the love of our child in my stomach. I open my mouth to tell him but nothing comes out. He wraps his arm around me and squeezes me closer.

"Let's have a baby," he whispers. I lift my head and look up at him, frowning slightly.

"What?"

"Let's have a baby. I know it's early, and I know we just got away from my family, but Sam, you're the one for me. I want to be with you forever and I want to have a child with you. I don't see the point in waiting. If you want to, obviously. I can wait." He bites his lip. "I don't know why I said that. Fuck, you probably think I'm a weirdo," he laughs. "I'm sorry. I just love you so fucking much."

I laugh. "Well yes, I do think you're a weirdo. But that's beside the point." We stare at each other for a few moments and I take a deep breath.

"What if I told you we are going to have a baby?"

He smiles. "I don't mean eventually, Sam. I mean let's have one soon. Let's have one now. Get off the pill and let's start trying."

I shake my head. "I don't mean eventually either." He frowns slightly and I smile gently. I have to whisper the words that have been on my mind ever since Jess and I went to the doctor.

"I'm pregnant, Dean."

His jaw drops open and his eyes widen. Suddenly a smile breaks out across his face and he starts laughing.

"What! No. Really?" I nod and he laughs again. "Why didn't you tell me!"

"I didn't want your parents to use it against you or me, and then I was afraid you'd freak out." I smile. "So you're happy?"

"Happy? I'm fucking ecstatic! Sam! We're going to be parents! I'm going to be a dad!"

I laugh as he wraps his arms around me and turns me onto my back. He dips his lips towards mine and kisses me so tenderly that I can feel the love radiating between us.

He pulls back and stares into my eyes, smiling as he runs

his hand over my stomach. I smile and put my hand over his. I still can't quite believe that we're here, together. I still can't quite believe that I'm this lucky. I wrap my arms around his neck and kiss him one more time. He nuzzles my nose with his and I laugh.

He's mine, and I'm his. This is what happiness feels like.

EPILOGUE

SAMANTHA

My hands are shaking as I tear open the envelope. I pull out the letter and scan my eyes over it before letting out a sigh and smiling at Dean.

"I'm officially divorced."

He smiles triumphantly and wraps his arms around me. "Good. I can make an honest woman out of you now."

"Not so fast," I laugh. "I'm not going to jump into another marriage without some serious thought."

"I can wait," he says, running his fingers over my growing belly. He kisses me gently and then pulls away and claps his hands together. "We should celebrate!"

I nod and he grabs a couple glasses. "Sparkling apple juice for you, wine for me," he says with a grin. I clink my glass against his and take a sip before tilting my head to the side.

"How did you get Ronnie to agree to the new terms? What did you say to him? He gave me everything in the settlement, way more than half."

Dean glances towards me and smiles sadly. When it came time to file the divorce papers for real, Dean called Ronnie's lawyer. During the final meeting he took Ronnie aside and got a whole new set of papers drawn up. I don't know what they said to each other, but I do know that Ronnie came back like a dog with a tail between his legs.

Dean takes another sip of wine and shrugs.

"I told him that my mother wouldn't protect him anymore. She obviously told him to get lost. He believed me."

"I still can't believe he was working for her," I say, shaking my head. "It's like a bad dream. The whole thing. From the moment I found out he wasn't being faithful to the final signature on those papers. Just a bad dream."

"But now," Dean says, running his fingers down my cheek and back towards my hair. "Now it's like winning the lottery."

I smile and tilt my head up towards him. He kisses me and I can taste the wine on his lips. I stare into his eyes and feel nothing but love and happiness overflowing in my heart. I run a hand over my stomach and look down at it before taking another sip of sparkling apple juice.

"I don't know how I got so lucky," I breathe. He kisses me softly until his phone rings to interrupt us. He looks down at the screen and makes a noise.

"Hey Pat, how did it go? Uh huh, great! That's great! Okay. Yep, talk to you later." He ends the call and looks at me, eyes shining.

"The kids loved the clown school. Apparently Margaret asked him if he could do it once a week. Pat was over the moon, he's been wanting to have a partnership like this ever since I met him."

I grin and wrap my arms around Dean.

"Thank you for making it work," I say. "I couldn't have convinced Margaret to give it a chance without your help. It'll be such a good addition to the program."

Dean shrugs. He looks at me curiously and then opens his mouth and then closing it again before speaking.

"I was thinking," he says slowly. "Since my family gave me access to the trust fund again, I have all this money. We've really struck a chord with the kids. What if we expanded the organization? We could try to get some federal funding and put some real money into the programs and get multiple locations in the city. We could get Pat and Margaret involved and make something real out of this. Have regular clown school classes in addition to all the programs you have already."

My eyes widen and I stare at Dean. "You mean you'd stop the investment banking?"

Dean nods. "Go full-time clown," he says with a grin. "There's so much potential to do good things here. Those kids love you, they love Margaret, and they love the clown classes. There are thousands more kids that could benefit from it. We could do it, Sam. We could make something great out of this."

I throw my arms around Dean and laugh as he swings me around. If my heart felt full before, it feels like it's absolutely about to burst. I stare at his face and shake my head.

"You never stop surprising me," I say in amazement.

Dean shrugs and turns towards the counter. When he turns back around he's got a big red nose on. He jumps up and spreads his palms wide with a big smile on his face and I can't help but laugh.

"Full-time clown," he says with a laugh. "Get used to it."

"Wouldn't want it any other way," I reply as I wrap my

arms around him again. I give his big red nose a squeeze before pressing my lips to his and once again tasting the sweetness of his kiss.

∼

I hope you enjoyed Knocked Up by the Billionaire's Son! I'd love it if you left a review to let me know what you think.

Get access to the Lilian Monroe Freebie Central to get bonus chapters from all my books!
All you have to do is go to http://eepurl.com/ddxnWL

∽

xox Lilian
www.lilianmonroe.com
Facebook: @MonroeRomance
Instagram: @lilian.monroe

Psst... Keep reading for your preview of Book 1 in my Mountain Man series:
Lie to Me

A Bad Boy Mountain Man Romance

LIE *to me*

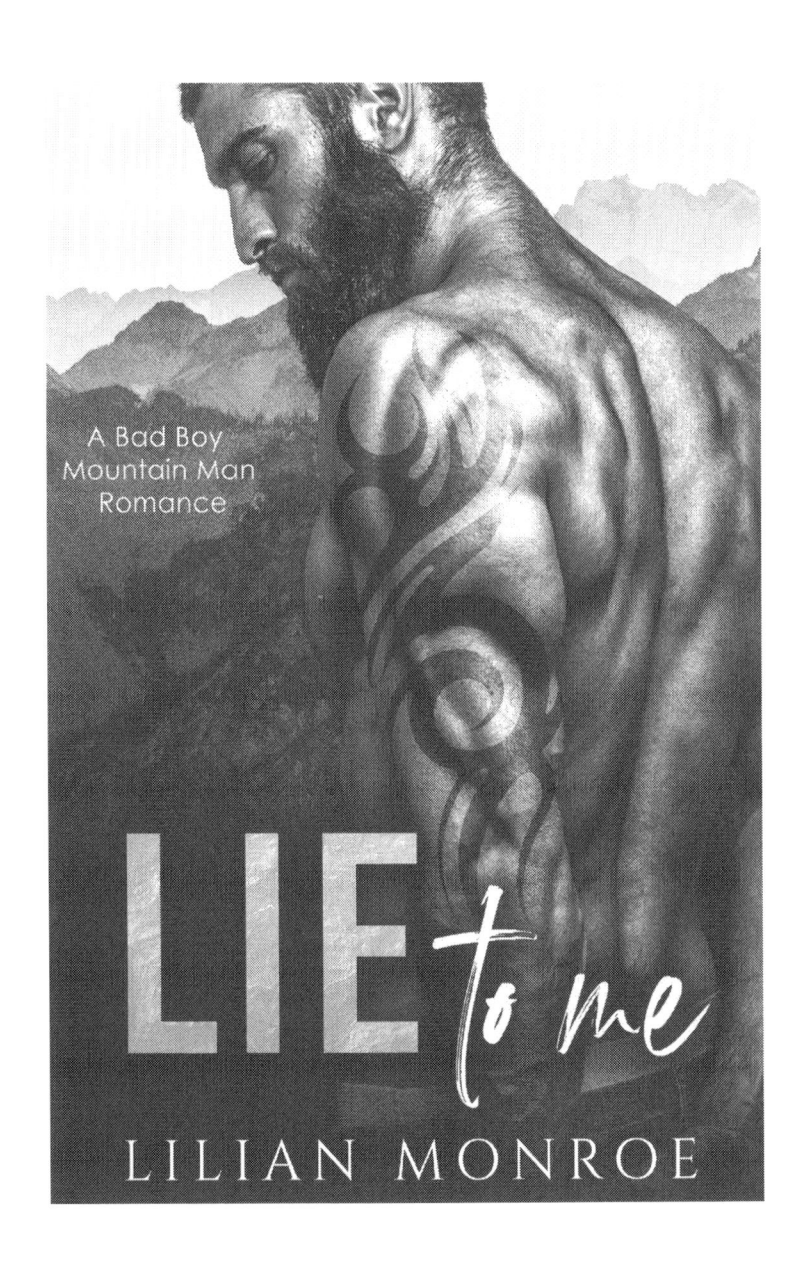

LILIAN MONROE

She's supposed to be my enemy.
And I'm supposed to hate everything about her.
But every time I see her, hate is the last thing on my mind.
Want, yes. *Need*, maybe. But *hate*? Not even a little bit.

I want her so much it's tearing me apart.
Soon, it might tear the whole town apart, too.
Right now I'm only sure of one thing: I'm in trouble.

He's supposed to be my enemy.
But *enemy* isn't how I'd describe him.
Rugged and mysterious? Yes. Irresistibly sexy? Absolutely.
One hundred percent, definitely, completely off-limits?
Yes, *yes,* ***yes!***

Aiden Clarke is turning my world upside down.
This is supposed to be work, just another normal job.
But ever since I got to this town, nothing seems normal anymore.

I can close my eyes and pretend that everything will be okay.
I can lie to myself.
I can believe all the lies that he wants to tell me.
Even though there's no way out of this, maybe we'll get our happily-ever-after.

Or maybe, these schoolgirl fantasies will crumble and burn right before my eyes.

Lie to Me is Book 1 of the Clarke Brothers Series. If you like rugged mountain men and sizzling hot heat, you'll love Lie to Me. Grab your copy today to find out if Maddy and Aiden get their happily-ever-after!

LIE TO ME

A BAD BOY MOUNTAIN MAN ROMANCE

Lilian Monroe

MADELINE

"Madeline! My office, now!"

I glance up from my desk and sigh. Barry isn't in a good mood. We're mobilizing to the new construction site next month, and there are a million things to do. I click 'save' on my computer and stand up. My environmental report will have to wait. I turn towards Barry's office and try to keep my face neutral.

Our project director, Barry Atkins, is a middle-aged, gruff-looking man with a big pot-belly. He's hunched over at his desk, squinting at his computer when I walk into his office. His eyebrows are knitted together and he's stroking his thick mustache with one hand as he scrolls down the screen with the other.

"Read this," he barks without looking up. I take a few steps to walk around his desk and look at his screen with him. It's an email forwarded on from our community liaison manager at the project site.

Town Hall Meeting

All residents of Lang Creek County are invited to the Town Hall Meeting at Lang Creek Community Centre, this Friday at 7:00pm. The construction of the Williamson Luxury Hotel on Lang Creek Mountain will be discussed. Please attend for any and all questions and comments.

Lang Creek Town Council

Barry glances at me and I take a deep breath. He shakes his head.

"The pushback we've been getting from the community is getting worse. They don't want this hotel to be built. I need you to go to Lang Creek and be the company representative for this town hall meeting."

I make a choking, gurgling sound before taking a deep breath.

"Barry, with all due respect, I have three applications to make to state and federal environmental agencies that need to be in by the end of next week. I don't have time to go down there, not now. If I don't get these submitted, we won't be able to start on time. Wouldn't it be better for one of the project engineers to go?"

"Who, Patrick? Glen? They'll make things worse! They'd go in there like they were ordering some workers around on site. No, we need someone with finesse." He looks at me and softens his voice. "We need you. You're the environmental engineer on this project and you're in the best position to put the community's mind at ease. We need to win their hearts and minds. Put a presentation together, and make sure you mention all our sustainability initiatives. Talk about that other project you worked on—the rehabilitation of the old mine site."

He waves his hand and I take a deep breath to try to calm myself down. I know how important this is, but as the only environmental engineer on this project, my plate is already too full.

"Barry, I need help. We're building this hotel on a Class 1 Nature reserve, and I have seventeen applications that need to be approved. The three going in next week are going to determine whether we can start on time. I can't—"

Barry swings his eyes up towards me and furrows his brow. I know that look. It's a look that doesn't invite discussion. I gulp and then nod, taking a deep breath to steady my voice.

"I'll get it done," I say.

Barry nods. "Good. I knew I could count on you."

He turns back to his computer and I head back towards my desk. I flop down on my chair and look at my computer screen, dejected. I have a half-finished Noise and Vibration Report, plus a to-do list that's overwhelming to look at. I look around at everyone tapping away on their keyboards and I wonder if they're as overwhelmed as I am. Now he wants me to put together a presentation *and* head into the heart of the Appalachian Mountains? I somehow have to win over the Lang Creek County population by Friday? What is our community liaison officer even doing down there!

I've worked with Barry for almost five years now, and I know that he's right. We need to handle the community correctly to save ourselves trouble down the line. But still, sometimes I feel like he relies on me too much. I pull out my Tupperware box from my bag and open it up. Looks like it'll be another lunch eaten alone at my desk as I rush to finish yet another task.

I haven't even stuck my fork into the salad leaves when

my phone rings. I check the screen and sigh. It's Cecilia, our community relations manager.

"Hi Cecilia," I say as I put my fork down and stare blankly at my screen.

"Maddy! Barry told me you'd be leading this town meeting."

"Not sure about leading it, but I'll be there."

"Have you prepared the presentation yet?"

"Cecilia, I just got told I'm going to Lang Creek ten minutes ago. I haven't even opened up PowerPoint yet." I can hear the tension in my voice and I try to take a quiet breath.

"Right, right. I've been having some issues getting people on board," she starts. "They're worried about the hotel construction site to begin with. Then they think it'll bring in too many tourists and the area will be destroyed."

I can tell. "I'll let you know when my presentation is done," I answer curtly. I hang up the phone and rub my hands over my temples. My lunch looks unappetizing, but I stab it with my fork anyway. I munch on a lettuce leaf before looking at my screen. I open up a blank presentation and take a deep breath. I might as well get started working on this.

AIDEN

I take a step back and run my eyes over the big pile of neatly stacked firewood. The sweat is beading on my forehead and I can feel it dripping down the center of my back. I unzip the front of my jacket and let the cool air come close to my body. I take a deep breath and nod to myself. This should keep me going for a month at least.

As I'm turning towards the cabin, I hear the crunch of car wheels on the gravel road leading up to my property. My eyebrows knit together and I walk towards the sound, ready to intercept whoever made the long, winding drive up to talk to me. They're either lost, or something is wrong. I don't get many visitors that come up just for a chat.

The familiar Lang Creek County Police emblem comes into view on the side of a white pickup truck. I stand at the top of my drive and wait for Sheriff Whittaker to stop the car and get out. He raises his arm towards me as he slams the pickup door closed.

"Aiden! How are you!"

"I'm fine, Bill. What brings you all the way up here?"

"Can't a man come and see his friend and make sure everything is all right? I haven't stopped by the garage in a while."

I nod with pursed lips. I don't like being reminded of work, and I spend as little time there as possible.

Bill walks towards me and extends his hand. I grasp it and we pump our arms up and down before he claps me on the back with his other hand.

"Good to see you're still alive, friend."

I nod towards the cabin. "Drink?"

Bill hesitates and points his thumb at his truck. "I haven't got much time today, Aiden. I'm on duty in town. There's actually something I wanted to talk to you about."

I nod slowly. I can feel that empty feeling in the pit of my stomach when I know there is bad news coming. My mind races to my brothers—did anything happen to them? Surely Bill wouldn't be in such a good mood if it did? I stare at him until he nods and opens his mouth to speak.

"There's a town hall meeting this Friday," he starts.

I shake my head. "Not interested." I turn towards the cabin and start walking away from Bill. His footsteps crunch as he jogs towards me.

"Aiden, wait! You've heard of the new hotel, haven't you? They're sending a representative to tell the town about it. We're going to vote on the construction. Your property runs alongside the hotel grounds for at least four acres. If anyone should have a say, it's you."

I stop and turn towards him. "You already know what I think about that hotel, Bill," I growl. Bill nods and takes another step closer to me. He spreads his palms up towards the sky and pleads with his eyes.

"Aiden, the town is divided. I agree with you, I don't think the hotel should be there, but what can I do? I'm the Sheriff, for Christ's sake. I need to be at least somewhat neutral. We need you to speak your mind."

I stare at his eyes and feel myself harden. My body becomes stiff and my gaze gets hard and cold. Bill stands his ground, staring into my face as I feel that familiar current of anger and resentment fill me up. I shake my head and turn back towards the cabin.

"Get one of my brothers to go," I call back. "I'm not interested."

"I can't!" Bill says. "Ethan is gone for Park Ranger training and Dominic... well, you know how Dominic is."

"So all that's left is me, is that it? Last resort?" I ask as I glance over my shoulder. Bill grins and shrugs his shoulders.

"Something like that."

I hesitate. If my brothers can't make it to town, no one will have the courage to speak up against the construction of the hotel. It's endorsed by the McCoy family, and they own half the town. Every time I pull on my coveralls to go to work with 'McCoy Trucking' branded across the chest, I almost shudder with disgust.

If this hotel gets constructed, the whole county will change. The virgin forest that surrounds us will be destroyed by droves of tourists and the quiet, sleepy town that I've always known will be overrun. My family's property will be the first to be impacted. I can hear my father's voice in my head telling me to go to the meeting. It's my duty to protect these forests.

But then I think about driving into town. I think about seeing Mara McCoy's mother at the town hall meeting and the way she'll look me up and down and lift her lip in a disgusted snarl. I shake my head.

"I'm busy, Bill. Get someone else."

I see Bill's shoulders slump before I turn back towards the cabin. I listen as his footsteps walk away from me towards his truck and hear the truck's motor start. I open the door to the cabin and walk inside without looking back. With a deep breath, I bring my hands up to my face and blow out all the air from my lungs.

I peel my jacket off and toss it towards a chair before kicking my work boots off. It only takes a couple steps before I'm in the kitchen. I rip the refrigerator door open and crack a beer. The cold liquid runs down my throat and by the time I put it back down, half of it is gone. I set the beer on the counter and wipe my lips on the back of my hand. My eyes drift up through the kitchen window. The corner of the big house is just visible through the trees. A pang goes through my heart and I shake my head.

I was supposed to be there, with a wife and kids, living the way my father taught us. I wanted to fill every one of the four bedrooms with children and teach them everything I knew. I wanted to smell warm cooking coming from the luxurious kitchen and know that I had a good woman beside me.

That never happened though.

Mara and her family betrayed us, and now I'm here. I'm living in a tiny cabin working for the family that took everything from my brothers and I.

The small cabin at the back of the property is all I need. I don't need a big house, or a woman, or children. I don't need to be involved in the town's problems. It doesn't matter if they build a hotel or not. It doesn't concern me. I finish my beer in one more gulp and toss the empty bottle into the trash. My eyes drift up towards the big house and I feel a shiver curl up my spine.

What will happen to it when the hotel is built? Will anyone come snooping through these woods? I shake my head. I know they will, and the little slice of peace that I've found up here will be gone forever.

MADELINE

I COLLAPSE onto my sofa when I get to my apartment. I try to turn my brain off, but it's still buzzing with all the things I have to do. I empty my purse and put my work phone and personal phone on the coffee table before slowly getting up to get myself a glass of water. I don't have the energy to make dinner tonight.

I only have three days before I need to leave for Lang Creek, and all three days will be completely packed with work. It seems to be the only thing I ever do anymore.

From the kitchen I hear my phone ring. I know it's my personal phone from the ringtone, and my heart sinks. The only person that would be calling me at this hour is my mother. I amble back to the living room and pick up my phone, sighing one last time before picking up.

"Hi, Mom," I breathe.

"Madeline! I have been trying to get through to you all day!"

"I was at work," I answer, my voice more terse than I mean it to be.

"Are you still doing that? Why don't you come and work for your father, dear? The hours will be much more manageable."

I bristle. We've been through this a million times, and a million times I've told her that I don't want to work for my father. The main reason I went into environmental engineering was to get away from the complete destruction of the oil and gas industry.

"Did you need anything, mom?" I ask.

"Yes! Pack your bag, you need to stay with us this weekend. Your father's doctor ordered him to go down to warmer weather, and with Bianca's new baby I thought it would be a great excuse to have a family vacation. I've booked a floor at the Ritz in Miami."

I try not to sigh audibly. "I have to work, mom, remember? My job? I'm going out to site this week. I can't cancel it."

My mother's exaggerated sigh comes through the phone. "This *job*! It's taking over your life. If you were just sensible, and..."

"I don't want any handouts—job, or money, or otherwise. I already live in this ridiculous luxury apartment in the middle of Manhattan that's way too big for me. I *don't* want to work in an industry that destroys the earth."

My mother is silent, and I can imagine the expression on her face. It's probably that perfect mix of outrage and disdain that she carries so well.

"Fine. Your father will be heartbroken," she answers.

"He'll live," I shoot back. I immediately regret my words when I hear a strangled sound come from my mother. With my dad's health declining, it's not the type of phrase that I should be throwing around.

"Sorry," I finally say. "I wish I could come, I really do. I just need to be on site this week."

"Well alright. Be careful."

The phone clicks and I lean back in the sofa. I let out all the air from my lungs and close my eyes. My hands come up to massage my temples as I try not to let the frustration bubble up inside me.

She's right.

I hate the voice in my head but I can't deny it. She's right. I'm working too much, and Dad is sick. I shouldn't be spending my time in Lang fucking Creek, I should be taking all the time I have to spend with him. I don't know how much longer we'll have together.

Maybe I should have just worked with him all these years. Maybe my pride and independence was misplaced, and I should have been grateful. After all, there are certain opportunities that only come with having a last name like Croft.

I remember being a kid and hating the way other kids at school looked at me. We all came from wealthy families—private school kids usually do—but my father made a name for himself with his extreme wealth. They looked at me with that unmistakable mix of respect and jealousy. I could see it from the time I was old enough to understand what jealousy was, and I vowed to myself that I wouldn't live my life riding on my parent's coattails.

And I haven't. Well, I've gotten myself an education with their help, of course. And my mother insisted on buying this apartment, but apart from that I've kept my father's identity a secret from my coworkers and bosses. To them I'm just Madeline Croft, the environmental engineer. I'm not Madeline Croft, the daughter of the oil and gas mogul.

I open my eyes and glance over at the shelf. I get up

slowly and walk over towards the old picture frame. The four of us: me, my sister Bianca, my father and mother. We're all smiling from ear to ear. The scintillating blue waters and bright white buildings of Santorini, Greece splay out behind us.

I grab the frame and stare at my father's face, brushing it gently with my finger. I was only eleven when we went on that trip, but I remember it like it was yesterday. Dad brought me out on a boat and taught me how to fish and I caught a massive red snapper. I still remember the pride in his eyes when we brought it back to shore. He told me I had a gift, and I'd be successful in whatever I chose to do.

The picture frame goes back on the shelf and I blink back the tears in my eyes. I wonder if he still thinks I'm successful? I wonder if when he said that, he was expecting me to take over the family company. I wonder if now, when he sees me, he still sees that girl with a world of possibilities ahead of her.

Maybe he just sees another engineer working for a big company moving up the ladder all too slowly.

I should be with him. I should be going to Miami, but instead I'm heading off into the wilderness. I sigh and turn away from the photo, shaking my head.

I can't think like this. He still has a long time ahead of him, and I have a long time to be with him. It's just one family trip, and I'm at an important point in my career.

I'm making the right choice by going to Lang Creek. I know I am. Maybe if I keep telling myself that I'll start to believe it.

AIDEN

My head is stuck under the hood of my father's old Chevrolet when I hear a car coming up the drive. I sigh. I hope this isn't Bill again.

I put down the wrench in my hand and grab my grease rag to wipe my hands with. Turning slowly, I lean against the front of the truck and watch the bend in the driveway for the approaching vehicle. My eyebrows inch upward when instead of seeing the Sheriff's pickup, I see my brother's truck rounding the corner.

He pulls up beside me and kills the engine before hopping out of the pickup. I push myself off the front bumper and walk towards him. The driver's side door swings open and I see Dominic's lumbering body come into view. He grunts and nods his chin down at me.

"Got those parts you asked for," he says, nodding his head towards the truck's flatbed.

"I'll help you unload them," I answer. We walk in silence towards the back of his truck where he opens the gate. I nod in appreciation. "Thanks, Dominic," I say. I've been trying to fix my father's old Chevy for weeks, and these look like they'll do the trick.

Dominic just grunts in response. I steal a glance his way and think of Bill's words. I'm not surprised he didn't ask Dominic to represent the town in the upcoming meeting. Physically, my brother is imposing. He's even bigger than me and I've always been built like an ox. But he is a man of few words, and the likelihood of him standing in front of a room full of people and voicing an opinion seems almost impossible.

I help Dominic unload the parts and nod in approval when I pick up the alternator.

"Where did you find this?" I ask. "I thought they didn't make these anymore. None of our suppliers at work had any."

Dominic shrugs and drops his load on the work bench in the garage. "Scrap yard," he explains. I nod and check the other things he's brought. A smile plays on my lips and I glance at my brother.

"This should do it. I'll have it up and running within the week," I tell him with a grin.

Dominic nods and starts walking back towards his truck. He pauses when he gets to the door, lifting his eyes up towards me and knitting his eyebrows together.

"You going to that town hall meeting?" he asks.

The question surprises me. It surprises me that he knows about the meeting in the first place, and it surprises me that he'd expect me to go. It's my turn to knit my brows together and I shrug.

"Not my business," I answer. Dominic's gaze hardens and he searches my face. I resist the urge to look away, keeping my gaze steady on my older brother. He used to look at me like this when we were kids, and it took me years to learn to keep eye contact.

"It is because of the McCoys?" he asks. Again, I'm surprised at his words. I don't remember the last time Dominic asked me an open-ended question about something other than cars and home maintenance.

I crack and finally look down at the gravel between us. My eyes search the rocks for an answer and I can feel my brother's gaze boring into me. I shrug.

"It's just not my business. Got nothing to do with them. I work for them, remember? It's not like I'm afraid of running into them."

"Dad wouldn't have wanted it," he says. "The hotel." I glance up at him and see a flash of something in his eyes. It looks almost tender, and then in an instant it's gone. He grunts at me and swings the door open, sliding his massive body behind the steering wheel. I watch him reverse and drive away before letting out a sigh.

I don't know what's inside me—frustration, maybe. Anger, even. Why does it have to be me that represents the town? There has to be someone else in town that can speak up against the new hotel!

As soon as the thought crosses my mind, I know there's no one. No one except us owns as much land as the McCoys. No one else has the weight of generations of family living in the area.

As much as I know it has to be me, I hate the thought of it. I hate the thought of driving into town when it's not absolutely necessary. I hate the thought of seeing those familiar streets and swallowing all the bitter memories that come with it.

I'm happy up here on my own. I don't need anything else.

This mountain, these forests—it's all I need. The reason I came up here and the reason I stay up here is to get away from Lang Creek and all its problems. Sure, I took a job at the garage, but I hardly have to drive into town to go there. The McCoy Trucking maintenance yard is on the way into town, so most days I don't even need to see anyone on my way in.

My eyes drift up towards the empty old house. I can just see the corner of it through the trees. I haven't been up there since I moved out after Dad died and it's almost completely overgrown. The cabin that I live in looks like a shack next to it and I shake my head.

I know that Bill is right. I know that Dominic is right. I have to go to the town hall meeting. I have to fulfill my promise to my father and protect these forests with every ounce of strength that I have.

If not for me, if not for the forest, then I have to do it for the memory of my father. I run my fingers over the car parts, resting my index on the alternator. I pick it up and turn it over in my hand, glancing at the old car I've been working on.

What's the point of restoring this car in memory of my father if I ignore his dying request? What's the point of living up here if I won't try to keep these forests free from development companies who want to clear cut the entire mountainside?

My eyes drift one more time to my childhood home and I nod to myself. I'll go to the town hall meeting. I'll speak my mind and I'll do everything I can to stop this hotel being built. I owe it to this mountain, I owe it to this forest, and I owe it to my father.

MADELINE

It's almost three hours from the airport over to Lang Creek. I grip the steering wheel in my rental car and navigate the winding roads, going higher and higher up through the mountains. I peer through the windscreen at the jaw-dropping scenery that spreads out around me in all directions.

It may be a long drive, but I understand why my company wants to build a hotel here. The mountains are massive and awe-inspiring. After a few hours of head-swiveling and jaw-dropping, I finally see a sign that tells me I'm entering the town of Lang Creek. I slow the car down and glance out the windows, studying the old buildings and small-town charm. I definitely understand why we're building here.

The town is built in a valley between two mountains, with houses spilling up the lower slopes of the peaks. The main street runs directly between the mountains. I see the shop and small existing hotel just ahead.

I pull up outside the hotel and read the sign: McCoy's Hotel. I turn off the engine and take a deep breath. Tomorrow evening, I'll be facing the townspeople. I'll be telling them exactly what my company wants them to hear. I'll be trying to convince them to support the construction of a multi-million-dollar luxury hotel in the heart of their small town.

My eyes swing around to take in the small timber houses and the hand-made signs that line the shopfronts. My lips purse together. A small tendril of something starts to curl inside me.

Is it doubt? I've always thought that I was doing something good for the world as an environmental engineer. I'm on the side of the 'good guys'. That's what I always tell myself, anyway.

But now as I look at this little town, nestled between two mountains and surrounded by thick forest, I wonder if I'm doing the right thing.

I shake my head.

I can't think like that. It's just because I didn't want to come here, and I thought I should be with my father instead of in this place. Of course I'm doing the right thing. We're bringing business to the area, jobs, and cash flow. I'm here to make sure that it happens ethically and that the delicate ecosystem of these virgin forests won't be disturbed more than necessary.

Those are all good things. I'm one of the good guys.

I finally open the door and swing my legs out, stretching my arms overhead and cracking my back before grabbing my small suitcase out of the back seat. I take a deep breath and start heading towards McCoy's Hotel. With a big more preparation tonight and tomorrow, I should be ready for the town hall meeting. I'll be ready to convince the townspeople that they should be happy about this project.

A bell jingles as I walk into the hotel lobby and an older

woman looks up from the desk. A smile spreads across her face as she looks at me.

"You must be Madeline Croft," she says. "I've been expecting you. Was the drive okay?"

"The drive was great," I respond. "It's so beautiful over here."

"That's why we want to share it with the world," she answers. She smiles at me again and I can't help but feel like she's smiling a bit too hard. It's almost forced, or it's like the smile doesn't spread all the way to her eyes. She nods at me before shuffling some papers in front of her. The check-in process is quick, and I'm hit with a barrage of information on the area. She tells me what to do, where to go, what to avoid. I nod and try to absorb it all, taking the brochures and maps from her with a smile. She hands me a key and points towards the staircase.

"Just up the stairs to the left. Room number 206."

"Thank you, Mrs. McCoy," I say.

"Please," she says with another forced smile. "Call me Karen. Ask me if you have any questions whatsoever."

I smile and nod before turning towards the stairs. They creak as I walk up, and I glance down the bright hallway towards the numbers on the doors. Number 206 is the third door down.

It's a clean room, with a cozy quilt and fresh flowers in the vase. I drop my suitcase and let all the air out of my lungs as I look around the room. This is my new home for the next few days. I don't even know how long I'll be here. The way Barry was talking it sounded like it would be a few weeks.

My phone buzzes and I glance down to see a picture message from my mother. I open it up to see the family smiling at a beach resort. My father looks tired and ill and my heart squeezes as I look at the photo. I know that my mother is trying to make me feel guilty for choosing work over this vacation, but I refuse to give in. I need to do this for myself, and I need to pursue my career the way that I want to do it.

I send her a quick message back and tuck my phone away. It's time to get some dinner at the restaurant downstairs, and then one final practice run through my presentation. Tomorrow morning I'm visiting the construction site and meeting with Cecilia and the site team. I glance around the room one more time and take a deep breath. Whether I like it or not, this is my new home.

When I walk downstairs, I glance out the big bay windows at the front of the hotel. The mountain is lit up with the sunset and the sky is ablaze with colors. The tightness in my chest loosens slightly and a smile spreads across my lips.

It might not be a beach vacation in Miami, but it doesn't mean this place isn't gorgeous. Maybe my new home isn't so bad after all.

AIDEN

My father's truck rumbles to life in the driveway. I smile as I run my hands over the steering wheel. I still remember being a young kid bouncing on the passenger's seat as my father drove me through the winding mountain roads. Now it's me in the driver's seat, but it still feels like he's here with me.

I glance at my watch and nod to myself. If I leave now I should make it down to Lang Creek just as the town hall meeting starts. My heart starts beating faster at the thought of driving into town, but I put the truck in gear and start driving before I can change my mind.

The long winding roads are comforting in their familiarity. I drive slowly, taking my time and enjoying the feel of the truck underneath me. I've always loved this vehicle, and it feels great to have it running again. I shift gears as I get to the main road into town and turn towards Lang Creek.

The truck jerks and shudders underneath me. I frown, trying to accelerate. The truck shudders again and starts to slow. I shift gears again and try to get the vehicle moving, but it shakes one more time and completely shuts off. I coast for a few feet before slowing to a stop as I pull over onto the shoulder.

Fuck.

I take a deep breath and pop the hood. I can see some smoke starting to curl up from the motor and I already know I won't be able to fix this without any tools. I lift the hood up anyway and cough as a cloud of black smoke billows out towards my face.

I glance back up the road towards my cabin. It's twelve miles away. Lang Creek is three miles down the road. As much as I hate the thought of walking to town and asking for help, it's the only chance I have of getting this truck off the road tonight. And of course, just my luck, everyone will be at that town hall meeting to hear about it.

The hood slams shut and I take a deep breath, filling my lungs with cool mountain air before heading off towards Lang Creek. Every step makes my heart beat a little bit harder. I'm not sure I'll be able to speak up in front of everyone, in front of Karen McCoy, in front of all the people who know what happened between our families. Even though I know why I need to speak up, I still wish someone else would do it.

By the time I walk onto Main Street, the sweat is beading on my forehead and I've opened my jacket up to let the air cool my body. I can feel a droplet of sweat running down my spine and I wipe my forehead with my sleeve. I check my watch and curse under my breath. Not only am I going to be late, I'm going to burst in dripping with sweat and asking for a lift back up to my cabin.

It's not exactly the image of a strong opposition. I can almost hear the townspeople sniggering under their breath as I walk in asking for their help. I haven't asked for help in years.

When I was a kid, my father was respected in the town. People looked to him for advice and guidance for everything from car maintenance to mountain safety. He built most of the houses in town himself, and was almost the unofficial mayor of the town. When he died, it's like the whole town became fragmented. No one knew who to turn to for help, and the whole rhythm of life was disrupted.

Maybe that was just my fourteen-year-old perspective of it. My father the superhero was taken before his time. My boots stomp on the ground as I make my way towards Lang Creek. If it were up to me, I'd be heading in the opposite direction, moving away from all the memories that assault me whenever I go into town. If it were up to me, my father would still be alive and my brothers and I would speak to each other more.

If it were up to me, maybe I wouldn't be alone on that mountain all the time.

I shake my head to dispel the thought. I like being alone. I like working by myself, and hearing the noises of the forest as I fall asleep I like living on the mountain and seeing its beauty everywhere I turn. I like using my hands and feeling the cool air burn my lungs when I'm working hard outside. I like heading into my tiny cabin and sleeping in my single bed as if I were a hibernating bear.

I know that I like all these things, but as my steps take my closer and closer to the Lang Creek town hall meeting, I can't help but wonder how convincing I'll be. I know what I could say to oppose the construction of this hotel. I'd talk about my father's legacy, about protecting the mountains and worshipping their power over us. I'd talk about the thousands of birds and insects and animals that call these forests home. I'd talk about the plants that feed us and protect us from the harshness of the winters.

I'd talk about all those things, but right now, all I can think about is speaking up and seeing all the eyes telling me that I've failed my father. Whenever I see the McCoys, all I can think of is how they betrayed my father. Every day when I go to work at their maintenance yard, it's like rubbing salt in the wound.

I'm not the man that my father was, or at least they don't think I am.

My heart squeezes just as I pass the huge wooden sign that says 'Welcome to Lang Creek'. My father put up that sign. I used to feel pride every time we'd drive into town. Now all I feel is pain.

I can already see the lights in Town Hall. The meeting must be underway already. I take a deep breath and force myself to speed up.

It doesn't matter what Karen McCoy says, or what her daughter Mara did to my family. It doesn't matter that my father's gone, or that my brothers and I hardly speak anymore. All that matters is that this hotel will destroy everything my family believed in for generations. It'll destroy the sanctity of the mountains and make it impossible for life to go on as it has.

Those words are on repeat, playing over and over in my head until my jaw is set and my chin dips downwards. I plant my palm against the door and push it open, letting the warmth of the indoors wash over me. Voices filter through to me from the main hall, and I square my shoulders before heading in that direction.

Before I turn the last corner, I hear a voice I've never

heard before. It's sweet and melodic, and it makes my heart jump in my chest. My eyebrows knit together as I try to recognize it. With every step that takes me closer to the voice, my heart starts thumping a little bit harder. I can't even make out the words. Something about conservation, or the environment.

I turn the final corner and see the main hall – it takes all my self-control to stop my jaw from dropping. When I heard the project's environmental engineer would come to speak at the meeting, I was expecting to see an old man with a big pot belly, or maybe a young man with a big ego.

I wasn't expecting a woman.

I wasn't expecting a woman *like her*.

Her blonde hair is pulled back into a low bun, with wisps of it framing her face. She's got high cheekbones and full pink lips. From the back of the room, I can't tell what color her eyes are. She's standing with her shoulders back and her head held high as she flicks through a couple slides of her presentation.

The door slams behind me and I jump as the whole room turns towards the noise. The woman's eyes lift up towards me and for a brief instant we look at each other. Time stops, and the room is empty except for her and I.

I forget why I'm here, or what I'm supposed to say. I forget everything except the fact that she's the most beautiful woman that I've ever seen.

∽

Thank you so much for reading. You can get the full version of Lie to Me by finding me at
https://www.amazon.com/author/lilianmonroe

Don't forget, you can get exclusive access to bonus chapters for ALL my books.
http://eepurl.com/ddxnWL

∽

xox Lilian
www.lilianmonroe.com
Facebook: @MonroeRomance
Instagram: @lilian.monroe

Printed by Amazon Italia Logistica S.r.l.
Torrazza Piemonte (TO), Italy